unturned rubbles

A STANDALONE NOVELLA

SANA KHATRI

Unturned Rubbles
Copyright © 2024 by Sana Khatri
Cover Design by Sana Khatri

All rights reserved. No part of this publication may be reproduced or transmitted in any form or by any means, including photocopying, recording, information storage and retrieval systems, or other electronic or mechanical methods, without express written permission from the author, except in the case of brief quotation embodied in reviews and certain other non-commercial uses permitted by the Copyright Law.

This is a work of fiction. Names, characters, places, events and incidents are the products of the author's imagination. Any resemblance to actual persons, living or dead, events or locales is purely coincidental.

ALSO BY SANA KHATRI

Those Chance Encounters

Can We Pretend?

Presuming You

When Words Waver

Feathers That Bleed

For the love you crave and the love you have. For the passion you share and the passion you receive. For that special kinda bond you simply can't resist, and for the hearts so bold they empower you whole.

IMPORTANT NOTE

Hello, darling! Thank you so much for choosing to read *Unturned Rubbles*. I'd just like to let you know that this book is a novella, so the characters may not appear as fleshed-out in this story as they do in my full-length novels. *Unturned Rubbles* is a quick, no-strings-attached story I wrote because Cass and Nia just popped into my head one day and demanded I give them a book. Y'all know how these things go, amiright? So, sit back, relax, and have fun!

P.S. This book contains brief mentions of substance use and overdose, and suicide. If these topics are a trigger to you in any manner of the way, then please consider your comfort before venturing ahead.

Playlist

Search for 'Unturned Rubbles' on Spotify

- Sentiments – Jenaux, Bryce Fox
- Rubble – Thomasin Grace
- Do It All Again – Punctual, Jordan Shaw
- Boys Like You – Anna Clendening
- Said Too Much – Jessie J
- You Got Away With It – Brett Young
- Black Hole – Griff
- Never Forget You – Conor Maynard
- My Heart's Grave – Faouzia
- Ride – Chase Rice, Macy Maloy
- Desire – Calvin Harris, Sam Smith
- Never Really Over – Katy Perry
- Not Yet – Brett Young
- Castle – Clarx, Harddope
- Slow – Diviners, RIELL
- Crowded Room – Conor Maynard
- Lose This – Dylan Emmet

ABOUT THE AUTHOR

Sana Khatri is an International Bestselling author, an IT (Information Technology) graduate, a bunny momma, and a makeup junkie. She resides with her aunts, mother, and her younger brother in Mumbai, India. Because her dad is the one who initially motivated her to keep writing, she makes sure to ask him for book-related opinions and suggestions whenever she needs them. She is an unwavering reader, dreamer, and believer, and prefers to have a speck of reality in her fictitious stories.

Twitter & Instagram: @isanakhatri

PROLOGUE

Past

Sweat drips down her damp skin as her lips part in a silent cry. With her long, sun-kissed hair fanned out, her skin flush with color, and her ice-blue eyes flared, she looks like a portrait of raw, youthful beauty.

His movements are deep, achingly thorough. His cock stretches her perfectly; his fingers tease her breasts in sinful strokes.

She fists the pillow under her head tighter, and when he grins down at her – that roguish curve of his mouth that she loves so much – she cups the side of his face with a hand and rises to kiss him.

He groans, and starts pumping his cock into her harder, which causes a burning pressure to rise in her.

His brows furrow a little. "Nia…" he whispers her name as his bright brown eyes run over her naked body.

She smiles and begins rocking her hips to match his thrusts. "Let go, Cass," she says softly. "Come with me." She bunches his short, unruly brown hair in a fist and presses her mouth to his.

He stiffens above her in an attempt to not raise his voice, then wraps his arms around her body before fucking her faster.

Her broken moans stifle against them with each pump of his hips, and when she comes – when *they* come – her back arches against the mattress, just as his shoulders shake, and his nails dig into her delicate skin.

"God, Nia." He nuzzles against her neck. "That was so hot."

She lets go of a breathless chuckle. "It always is, isn't it?"

She's never known a touch like his. Never known a kiss that wasn't his. Never known a pleasure that wasn't given to her by him. Cass is her world, just as she is his.

Inseparable – they've been unbreakable ever since they shook hands all those years ago as kids when he'd moved into the house next to hers. Sleepovers, movie nights, study sessions – they did it all together.

Always together.

Her first touch, first kiss, first sex – he'd been it all, just as she'd been his.

Like a mantel and flame, like a siren and sea, they went together; they *fit* together.

Rose and thrashed and thrived together.

Nia bites her lower lip as she runs her fingers over his smooth jaw. "We gotta complete that Economics assignment," she says. It's why she'd walked next door to his house in the first place. Well, at least that's what she'd told herself an hour ago when she'd knocked on his door and his mom had answered it with a knowing smirk on her face.

Cass's expression – that was relaxed and satiated just a moment ago – shifts to something dark. Something that makes her stomach tighten.

"What is it?" she asks reluctantly.

He swallows and averts his gaze from her, then abruptly gets to his feet before heading into the attached bathroom.

With her eyes on the wooden ceiling, and her heart in her throat, she focuses on the noises around her as she waits for him to come back out.

The sound of him flushing.

Of the faucet running.

A cabinet opening and closing.

Then…

His footsteps on the floor as he walks out.

Almost tentatively, she watches as he puts on his discarded jeans and t-shirt, then let go of a limp breath when he sits at the edge of the bed with his back to her.

"I'm…*we're* moving to New York next month," he says. "Mom, Dad, and I." A muscle ticks in his jaw as he tries to control the suffocating anxiousness he's feeling right now.

She sits up and stares at him, not bothering to cover herself. Deafening silence breathes down her neck in the aftermath of his confession, and an irritable buzz of something foreign makes her feel dizzy.

"What?" The word is a pathetic excuse of a whisper. "What're you…" Her voice – it won't cooperate with her. She tries, but ends up failing to make herself speak.

How have things changed so drastically in just a matter of minutes?

Cass turns his head to the left, but still doesn't meet her eyes. "You know I've always wanted more, Nia – more from school, from people. From *Life*."

She grimaces when her eyes sting. "I do. But this… Cass, this is a decision you promised you'd make with *me*. You told me we'd go to college together. *Be* together. You wanted to graduate here; you wanted to be with me. You…you can't just…"

"I had an opportunity, and I didn't wanna let it pass." He finally looks at her. "My dad got a promotion and was asked to transfer to NYC. And he said yes, because he knows I've always wanted to go, and also because that city has so much potential for the entire family. I… Fuck, Nia, I just *couldn't* say no."

"But you *can* leave me here after making all those elaborate promises to me, making me believe in things that I otherwise wouldn't have put my faith in," she grits out, and when he doesn't reply, she scoffs and gets off the bed before hastily putting her clothes back on.

She sucks in a breath when her tears threaten to flow, and swallows the growing lump in her throat while fixing her hair into a ponytail above her head.

"Nia…" Cass voices slowly, but she refuses to glance his way.

"*Nia*," he says a bit firmly now.

She buttons her shorts and looks at him. "*What*, Cass?"

"Can we talk, please?"

She doesn't stop her anger from surfacing, her pain from showing on her face. "You've broken me, hurt me. You've betrayed *everything* I thought we had, just to fulfil your selfish desire of wanting to move to a big city. And I understand that you put yourself first in this situation, but there's something you need to understand, too, Cass. Just because you've decided to move on, doesn't mean I'll be onboard with the idea as well. I have the right to be upset, and I sure as hell reserve the right to not want to speak to you."

"Nia, come on. *Please*."

"I fucking *hate* you," she croaks out, and her tears finally spill out, tainting her cheeks and making her vision blurry. She puts a hand over her mouth as her emotions get the better of her, because the last thing she would have expected was to direct those 3 words at Cass. But damn it, it hurts, and the pain warrants a release – be it with anger or sadness.

Cass stands up so he can look at her fully, his own pain flashing openly across his features. "You don't mean that," he says, more to himself than her.

She sniffs and swipes her shaky fingers over her face. "Oh, but I *do*." She takes a step towards him, then thinks better of it and moves back. "Were you even going to let me know about it?" she asks. "If I hadn't mentioned the assignment, would you have told me? Why do you even come to school? What's the point of it if you're fucking *leaving* anyway?"

"You know I wouldn't have left without telling you," he states.

"Do I, though?" she challenges.

"Nia, please…" He tries to reach for her, but she jerks away from him.

"Don't," she warns, mainly to keep herself from falling apart. If he touches her, she knows she won't be able to stop him. And that's the kind of power she simply can't hand over, not anymore.

He clenches his hands at his sides. "What do you want me to do?" he questions, his anger rising. "What the fuck would you have me do, huh, Nia? Stay here in Adenbrooke – a lame-ass town in the middle of Maine with no hope of reaching my goals? Be as aimless and naïve and stupid as you, with no ambition in life other than selling coffee and pastries at your parents' café? Have no real motives other than marrying and having kids, and have them be just as foolish as you? Because that's not me; that's not even *remotely* close to who I am."

To say that she's shocked would be an understatement. To say that his words have gutted her would be a cruel joke.

"Wow…" she whispers, just as Cass's eyes widen in realization.

"*Fuck*," he spits out. "Nia, I swear I didn't mean–"

"Save it." She grabs her bag from next to his bed, then breezes past him and towards the door, only to stop when she reaches the threshold. "If you think I'm so dumb and useless, why did you tell me you loved me?" she asks, letting yet another tear paint her cheek. "Why did you kiss me on my porch last year and ask me to be yours? Why did you fuck me a week after and call me beautiful?" She doesn't want to cry, but it's hard not to when you're getting your heart broken by the man you thought was your forever.

Thirteen years of friendship, laughter, love, and *this* is what it's accounting to in the end. And what's worse is that he didn't even consider telling her about his decision until he absolutely *had* to.

Cass doesn't say anything; he doesn't know what to. He shot an arrow, but it ricocheted back to him, hitting him squarely in the chest.

"Was it because you had something to prove, Cass?" Nia questions softly. "To yourself, maybe, or to someone else. Is that what it was for you?"

"You know that's not what it is, baby. You know I love–"

"Goodbye, Cass," she says, her throat tight. "And good luck. May you get everything you're looking for, and your paths never cross with someone as aimless and naïve as me, because I wouldn't wish the pain I'm feeling right now on anyone."

As she walks away from him – from what he meant to her – she ignores his voice, his pleas. His desperation and regret. She ignores it all, and lets the battered pieces of herself fall to the ground – like timeless rubbles of a once-glorious empire raining down on an inevitable fate.

1.
nia

Present

11 years later

The heady, thick aroma of coffee wafts through my café's kitchen and out into the main area. It hits my eager senses, and I sigh as I ring a customer, hand them their order, then wave them goodbye.

After Mom and Dad decided to retire three years ago, they handed over *Café Connell's* reigns to me and my elder brother, Noah. The café has not only been a part of our lives – part of our family and legacy – from the very beginning, but it has also been a place where I've always found the most peace and contentment.

Handling a business, especially one as busy as ours, comes with a lot of challenges. The initial pressure and confusion, along with the fear of disappointing the trusted customers, *and* of letting our parents down – it all weighed heavily on Noah and I during our first year as *Café Connell's* owners. But, where he became the brains behind things, I quickly turned into the source of engagement and presentation. I've never doubted our partnership, but to see it come to life every day at the shop – it's a dose of thrill I'll always crave more of.

Adenbrooke isn't necessarily a crowded town. With a population of approximately 27,869, it might as well be a giant family living in a massive bubble or something. But despite all that, the café is always bustling with activity, either from new sit-in customers, or the screaming kids who come barging in with their parents, demanding pastries and chocolates. From workers on a rush, desperate for a cup of lifesaving coffee, or the nosy elderlies who want nothing to do with the things in the shop and everything to do with two-bit 'round-town gossip. It really is a joy to witness every flavor Adenbrooke has to offer, as eccentric as they may be.

I bring my long, dark-blonde hair over a shoulder, fix the sleeves of my pink turtleneck sweater, and turn around, only to find Noah seated in a chair behind the main counter, with a pile of papers in his hand and a frown on his face.

"Hey there, big guy." I smile as I walk over to him. "What's got you so focused this early in the morning?" I tap a long nail against a sheet of paper, then point at a drawer next to him.

He grabs my purple apron from said drawer before handing it to me, then looks up when I come to stand next to him. "My specialty: financial bullshit." He grins, making me chuckle.

I put on the apron while glancing at his lazily styled short hair – the color of it a replica of mine – and his clear blue eyes. "And how are we looking?" I ask, then straighten the collar of his black flannel.

His expression softens. "We're thriving, Nia; you don't have anything to worry about."

I exhale sharply. "I know. But it's just that–"

"You're scared of letting people down, I get it." He gets to his feet, and I have to look up to meet his sincere gaze. "We are *killing* it, and I'm not just saying that because we're badasses, but because it's *true*. We're working really hard and it's showing here." He jerks his head at the papers. "I'm so proud of what we've achieved together so far."

My shoulders slump a little as I relax into myself, and he chuckles.

"What?"

"You keep telling me that *I* worry too much, but really, it's the other way round."

I roll my eyes. "Well, at least *one* of us has to be the responsible one, right?"

"Hey, now. I'm older than you, remember?" He ruffles my hair, to which I step away from him with a scowl. "*Seven* years older. Treat me with some respect." He winks – or *tries* to, at least. He's never been able to do it right, and I doubt he ever will be.

"I'll show you respect the day you learn how to throw a proper wink," I muse.

He hums in mock contemplation. "Tough bargain, but I accept. Also, you gotta–" He stops and looks over my shoulders when bells jingle, and the café's door opens with a bang.

Customers gasp at the sudden noise, and when I pivot on my feet, I see a man with a lanky frame, shabby black hair, and dark eyes panting miserably as he makes his way to the counter. He's wearing a grey sweater and an oversized winter coat, and keeps apologizing to people as he goes. By the time he reaches Noah and I, he's even more out of breath than he was before.

"Hi, my name's Randall," he begins, then lets go of a sigh and rubs his gloved hands together before giving us a goofy smile. "Umm, I need 36 cups of coffee – black. Uh…" He briefly looks at the piece of paper he's holding. "Yeah, 36 cups. 2 sugars in 12 cups, no sugar in 2 cups, and 1 sugar in the rest."

I stare at him for a beat or two, then glance at my brother, whose face shows nothing but open amusement at our intriguing customer.

"Sure thing," I say, then grab Noah by the bicep before hauling him over to the coffee machines. "I'm not filling 36 cups myself. Get your ass into gear; put those muscles to use and all that shit."

He laughs airily. "You got it, *boss*."

My lips twitch.

"Who the hell needs 36 fucking cups of coffee on a Saturday morning anyway?" he asks incredulously, low enough so that Randall can't hear him.

I lift a shoulder and grab a new cup. "Satan and his band of misfits, maybe."

My brother tips his head back and laughs, and I grin as we fall into the rhythm of getting the outrageous order ready.

2.
cass

I'd forgotten how crisp and ass-biting the winters in Adenbrooke can be. It's very in-your-face, with the calming smell of snow and winter spruces, along with burning wood and fresh coffee. And the carb-dripping food you get here? It only adds a level of authenticity to the overall picturesque vibe. A trademark of sorts, meant only for this town.

11 years away from this place, and yet, my brain begins navigating the streets, shops, and bus stations with un-hiccupped ease. It kind of feels like I'd never even left.

Being a model, celebrity fitness trainer, and a YouTube influencer comes with its own set of opportunities. I have a solid career and financial stability, and I'm so fucking proud of myself for having achieved it all at the age of 27.

When I was offered a documentary series by Netflix three months ago, I jumped at the chance of unveiling more of myself and my personality to my audience and clients. Netflix is a *huge* platform, and the fact that I'm going to get my own show on it – it's an accomplishment that's beyond my wildest imagination.

I scratch my thick stubble and take off my black beanie, resulting in my shoulder-length hair to flow haphazardly with the icy wind. Sliding my hands into the front pockets of my dark jeans, I look around the large open space I'm standing in the middle of.

I'd told my manager, Amanda, that I wanted to film half the documentary in Adenbrooke, because I have so many memories and places here that I want to share with my fans.

The B&B we've booked for ourselves and the 34 crew members who will be helping me with the documentary, has a massive back area which is usually reserved for weddings and occasional town parties. I've decided to film bits of sit-down moments here, which is why the crew is currently hauling all the cameras and equipment out of our tour buses and onto the vacant ground.

"Randall, my man, what the ever-loving *fuck*?" says one of the crew members.

I turn and look at Randall, who is covered in snow and is standing next to an empty table. He carefully places four large paper bags on it, and the kid next to him does the same.

"Thanks, Davis," Randall tells him. "Couldn't have done it without you, buddy."

"My name's Dave," the kid corrects. "Where's the $20 you promised anyway? I didn't agree to help your whiny ass for free."

"I'm sorry, but did you just *curse*?" Randall asks. "Aren't you 12 or something?"

The kid rolls his eyes. "15, actually." He holds out a hand. "Money."

My lips twitch. I quickly tie my hair in a bun and walk over to the table, just as Randall hands the kid the promised cash.

"Thanks." He counts the money for good measure, then turns and walks away without a back-glance, leaving Randall dumbfounded in his wake.

I chuckle. "Only a few hours here and you've already been played," I say.

He straightens, despite looking utterly disheveled. "Sir."

I wave a hand at him. "Don't go all formal with me, please; it makes me uncomfortable." I glance ahead, and smile at Amanda when I see her walking over to me.

She jerks her chin at the paper bags, which results in her short, jet-black hair to sway to the right.

"Coffee?" she asks Randall.

He nods. "Yes, ma'am."

"Will you distribute them among the crew? Ask for assistance so it doesn't take long," she says to him. "And don't forget to grab your cup, too."

He gives her a grateful smile, then pulls out two cups from the 3rd bag before placing them on the table in front of us. He then calls out to a couple of crew guys to come help him with the bags, and as they all go around distributing the coffee, I reach out a hand to grab my cup.

I've only just wrapped my fingers around it when my entire body stiffens, and my heart almost races out of my chest when I see the logo printed on the center of the beige Styrofoam cup.

Café Connell

How many times have I seen this logo?

How many times have I absentmindedly traced my fingers over it during study sessions at the café?

Fuck…

How acquainted am I with the people who own the place?

How well I know them…

Know *her*…

Goosebumps mar my skin, and my neck heats at the memories of her. Of *Us*.

God…*her*.

"Cass?" Amanda's hand touches my left arm before she shakes me gently. "Cass, hey. You okay?"

I blink and look at her, then clear my throat and run a hand over my face. "I'm fine." I give her a clinical smile. "Sorry."

Her brows furrow in concern, but she sighs and doesn't question me further.

I turn to my right. "Yo, Randall!"

He faces me. "Yes, sir? I mean, uh, Cass…sir."

"Who took your coffee order?" I ask. I know Amanda is watching me, but I don't care. Despite being my manager, she doesn't know anything about *her*.

I haven't told *anyone*.

And I know I shouldn't ask Randall what I just did; that I shouldn't do this to myself right now. But fuck if I give a damn. I need to know. I just…*I need to know*.

"Uh…" Randall scratches his head. "It was this short blonde chick and a muscly guy."

My throat tightens. Her – it was her.

God… It was *her*.

"Thanks, man," I tell him, then glance at the coffee cup again. With a swallow, I grab it off the table and run the pad of my thumb over the logo. Had she touched this cup, or was it Noah who'd filled it?

I'm aware that I'm being absolutely stupid, but my rationality jumped off a metaphorical window the second I saw where the coffee has come from, so I can't exactly be expected to act sane anyway.

I clench my jaw and stare at my boots. I *knew* this would happen – knew that like the very air around me, she'd begin seeping into my skin the moment I stepped foot in Adenbrooke. I knew it well and thorough, and yet, like the fiend for punishment that I am, I decided to come back, to stay – if only temporarily.

That I decided to let Nia Connell breeze into my life once again and claim residence in that helpless, pathetic heart of mine.

3.
nia

"You're *27*, Nia. Try not to act so forlorn, will you?" says one of my friends, Laine.

"Exactly. You go around like there's no sense of purpose in your life or something," adds Dara, then waves a hand around us. "*Look* at this crowd, babe. It's filled with potential fucks. Find a hottie and ride him until he can't stand anymore."

"Juice him and then lose him, as I like to say," Emma chimes in with a wiggle of her brows, and I genuinely wish I was a violent human being, because I would love to strangle the fuck out of her for saying that.

We're at *Hazel's Bar* enjoying our usual Saturday-evening drinks. It's been our tradition ever since we graduated college, and one I hope to continue even when I'm a 90-year-old bag of skin and bones.

I scowl at Emma, because, well, violence is illegal and all that, then finish my glass of whiskey sour a little too aggressively. I'm about to comment on her lack of eloquence when it comes to having a decent conversation, but stop when I feel a presence – a familiar yet irking one – on my back, making my spine stiffen.

"Here looking for a one-night dick, Nia?" His deep voice slithers over me; his heated breaths all but burn my skin. "Looking for a cock that can finally knock you up?"

Laine, Dara, and Emma tense. I stop myself from doing the same, and turn in my seat before glaring at the man in front of me.

"*Brandon*," I spit his name with as much distaste as I can. "What I'm here for is none of your goddamn business."

His green eyes gleam as he steps closer to me. "You're my *wife*, you little–"

"*Ex*," I cut him off. "I'm your *ex*-wife, Brandon. Did you, or did you not, sign the divorce papers 3 years ago?"

He grits his teeth. "You know I didn't want to," he hisses close to my face. "You know I wanted you, but you wouldn't give me a fucking baby, and I couldn't–"

"Cut the crap, Bran," I tell him. "You know it isn't my fault that despite trying everything we possibly could, nothing ended up working for us. You know it wasn't in my hands, and yet you humiliated me in front of the whole town during that party; called me names that no husband should his wife. If you wanted me, you wouldn't have acted so savagely towards me." I swallow the sudden tightness in my throat. "You never really wanted me, did you? You just liked the *idea* of owning me." I gently push at his chest and get to my feet, then glance at the girls. "I think I'm going to call it a night. I'll see you guys later." I throw a $10 bill on the counter and start making my way to the door.

"Don't be a bitch, Nia. Are you seriously going to walk away from me right now?" Brandon calls out as he follows after me. He isn't drunk; I couldn't smell any alcohol on him. He's just naturally this disgusting, which only makes me further question my past choices.

I don't answer him, and only stop once I've reached the bar's wooden door. I yank it open and look up, and every part of me goes numb when I see *him* standing a few feet from me.

"You're a whore," Brandon sneers from behind. "You're a useless and weak woman who thought she could…"

I let his words fade, because standing before me – with a hand in front of him as if he was about to push open the door and enter the bar – is the painfully incomplete poem of my past. The boy – no, the *man* – in front of me is a vivid contradiction to the person I knew 11 years ago. He's a sculpture now perfected; a mold now solidified.

I would gasp, but his overpowering presence simply won't let me. I would try to breathe, but his brown eyes are currently holding me captive. I would will myself to move, but his parted lips have paralyzed me in place.

And, when he blinks and runs his wild gaze over me, I'm not sure if my heart is beating at all.

"Nia…" he whispers my name, and I swear to God my entire being crashes against the wave of his voice.

With Brandon now a forgotten piece of nothing, I finally let go of a breath and brave meeting Cass Madden's searching, all-too-familiar eyes.

4.
cass

She stares up at me like she's never seen me before. I don't blame her, especially because 11 years is a long time – enough to change anyone both mentally and physically. And, given how young we were when we last spoke, I am just as dumbfounded to see her standing in front of me – as breathtaking as ever – studying me like I'm a complete stranger, and not someone she once loved.

Nia blinks, and Christ if it isn't a trigger to my ticking senses.

Her hair is longer, wavier. The blue of her eyes is dimmer than I remember, and the once-prominent freckles on her cheeks were now lighter, like they've been airbrushed into subtlety. The lavender dress and leather jacket she's wearing perfectly complement the gentle curves of her lush body, and drive me insane to the point where I can't see straight for a moment.

"Are you even listening to me, you slut?" someone chides.

I whip my head up, and see Brandon Jones glaring at the back of Nia's head with a scowl on his face.

Anger sizzles in my veins. I take half a step forward and roughly grab the collar of his blue shirt. "What did you just call her?" I growl, and when he tries to free himself, I tighten my hold and rock him once before getting in his face. "*What the fuck did you just call her, Brandon?*" I feel the patrons watching my encounter with Mr. Dipshit Galore, but I ignore their mindless whispers.

"I don't have to answer you, Madden," Brandon says. "I can call her whatever the hell I want. She's my wife, you hear me? She's my–"

"*Ex*-wife, Bran. *Ex. Wife*," Nia states from my right.

I feel bile rising in the back of my throat. My rage simmers to ice; my palms turn clammy. The words, the *weight* of them, the truth of it – it makes me lose my hold on Brandon, who takes that as an opportunity to free himself.

"Took the ground right from under ya, didn't it?" he mocks with a vicious smile on his smug face. "You left her for New York, so her family picked *me* to look after her. To *marry* her. She may have been a sloppy second, but *damn* she's hot, and I enjoyed every bit of her b–"

I don't let him finish; I reel my right arm back and punch him in the jaw.

The fucker howls in pain, and I hear a satisfying *pop*, which is soon followed by the sound of him crashing against a table and falling onto the beer-stained floor.

A couple of guys help him to his feet, and when he looks at me with murder in his eyes, I sniff and flip him off.

Brandon gives me a once over, and realizes very quickly that he can't take me. Trembling in anger, he spits blood on the ground and walks past a shell-shocked Nia before heading for the bar's open door. The former high school jock, the wannabe "Mr. Cool," then *runs* out into the street like his ass just caught fire.

Some patrons snicker, whereas Nia? Well, she's frozen in place.

"Hey." I step in front of her. "Nia."

She sucks in a breath as she scans my face. "You punched him," she whispers, then swallows. "You…" She shakes her head in disbelief. "You really punched that dickwad."

I try not to smile, then test the waters by grabbing her left hand, and have to refrain from cursing when her silk-like skin brushes against my calluses. Christ, how I've missed the feel of her touches.

I deprived myself of her, but now that she's in front of me, I don't know how long it'll be before I break and take what I'm going mad for.

Nia watches our joined hands with hesitance on her face. I can see the conflict in her eyes, one where she can't decide whether to pull away from me, or to stay as is.

I don't wait for her to pick an option, merely because I'm scared I won't like it.

"Can I buy you a drink?" I ask her.

She looks up, opens and closes her mouth, but doesn't say anything.

"Perfect; I'll take that as a yes." I nudge her softly, then walk us over to the other side of the bar with a crazy-big smile on my face.

Man, it feels *good* to be back.

5.
cass

"It's a documentary series for Netflix," I tell Nia, then take a long swig of my beer. "The episode count is TBD at the moment, but I'm aiming for 8, max. Don't wanna drag it too much."

She sips her whiskey sour slowly, and I can't help but let my shameless eyes travel over her body.

She's changed so much, and yet, she's still the same girl I fell head over heels in love with all those years ago. That hasn't changed, of course, and the proof of it – it's inked on my skin like a brand of honor.

Sentiments, by Jenaux and Bryce Fox, starts playing, and I watch as Nia taps her feet and bobs her head in time with the song.

She likes Bryce Fox. Interesting. I store that bit of information in case I might need it.

"So… Hundreds and thousands of people will watch your documentary online, huh?" she asks tentatively, like her words aren't meant to be spoken.

She's trying to act casual, but I know it's hard for her, just as it is for me.

"That's what the creators and I are hoping for, yeah," I say.

"That's nice." She gives me a small smile. "I'm happy for you, Cass. You got what you wanted; you're successful and doing what you love. And that had been your goal from the very beginning, hadn't it?" Her eyes shine under the yellow lights of the bar, and I just…I lose myself in her. In her simplicity and elegance.

"God, you're so fucking beautiful, Nia," I tell her, and swallow when her chest rises and falls rapidly as she stares at me. "The first time I realized that, it was on your porch all those years ago on the night after our first kiss, and I…I almost fell on my knees in front of you. You took the sanity right out of me, and I was so helplessly in love that I didn't even care."

She inhales sharply and glances around fleetingly. "Cass, please…"

"Why did you pick Brandon, Nia?" I ask. "Why *him*?"

"It wasn't my choice to make." She snatches her glass from the counter and finishes it in one go. "Both our parents decided on it, so I just said yes. Brandon is stable. He has his own garage, and he earns really well from it. I didn't want to rebel and disappoint my mom and dad, so I…well, I said yes." She sighs and places the glass back on the counter. "But he wanted kids, and even after trying everything, we couldn't have any. He was getting sick and tired of hearing no, and 'The test says negative', so he just…exploded one day. Scolded and demeaned me at a town fair 3 years ago and said he was done." She sniffs, then laughs, but there's no humor in it. "And I don't know what came over me, but I looked him in the eye and said: "Good riddance. I'll send the divorce papers your way ASAP." He stomped away without saying anything, and that was the end of us."

I polish off the rest of my beer in order to get the image of Brandon and Nia having sex out of my head. I know she's watching me, know that she can see how I'm choking the ever-loving fuck out of the glass bottle, hoping it was Brandon's neck instead, but I don't hide my anger.

It's all your fault, you dipshit, says a voice in my head. *If you hadn't left, things would have been very,* very *different now*.

It's an easy truth, of course, but one I can't fully digest due to my lack of general common sense.

I lick my lips and tap my fingers on the counter. "Why couldn't you have kids with him?" I brave asking.

She pushes a strand of hair behind an ear as she eyes her lap. "Lack of sperm count."

"But that's *his* fault, not yours."

She shrugs. "The doctor asked us to keep trying unless we really *had* to resort to medications, but I guess Bran was done making fruitless attempts."

I shake my head. "I knew he sucked at being a decent human being, but didn't realize he was incapable of being a full-blown man, too."

Nia places a hand over her mouth as she coughs, most probably to mask her laughter. "That's…not a very kind thing to say. His flaws are his to endure. We shouldn't make fun of them."

I smirk. "Admit it, though: he deserves it," I muse.

"Maybe…" She smooths a hand down the front of her dress. "But I think that knowing the truth has made him far more bitter than he was before. He's more inconsiderate now, more…I don't know…"

"Bitchy?" I provide. "Nia, he's always been a dick. And for someone like him, there's no redemption – only the scorching flames of hell, and a trident sharp enough to pierce his pompous ass into oblivion. Or whatever the hell-equivalent of oblivion is."

She laughs – the sound loud yet sweet – then clicks her tongue. "I'll have to agree with you here."

I chuckle, and she meets my eyes before an almost regretful sort of expression takes over her face.

"Uh, I should go," she states all of a sudden, then gets to her feet. "I have an early day tomorrow."

I raise a brow. "On a Sunday, when the café stays closed?"

She hesitates. "I have other plans."

Liar, I want to say, but don't. Instead, I stand and step closer to her. "Let me walk you to your car."

"I don't have a car."

"Then how did you get here? Did someone give you a lift?"

Real smooth, Cass, I tell myself. *You don't* at all *sound like a weirdo with stalker tendencies.*

"I walked here, actually," Nia answers. "I came here to meet my friends for our weekly drink sesh, but they left a few minutes ago, so it'll be me and my feet again."

"I can drop you home." The words could *not* have left my mouth any faster than they did. Again, *real smooth* on my part.

Nia waves a dismissive hand my way. "That's fine. It's a short distance away anyway, so I don't really need a ride."

"It's Saturday night, and the streets are full of drunk idiots, Nia. I know it's a small town, but that doesn't mean you don't have assholes here. Also, you have a couple of drinks in you, and it's snowing outside. I don't want you to hurt yourself, or worse, get lost or something."

She jerks her head back and gives me an incredulous look. "I know my way around, Cass, thank you very much. How, you ask? Because I've been here the whole time! In case you forgot, it's not *me* who left; it was you. *You* left. *You* decided to let go and move elsewhere. So no, I *won't* get lost; I *won't* get attacked by some random drunk on the street. And you know why that is?" Anger brushes its fingers over her features. "Because I'm no longer that stupid and naïve girl you ditched 11 years ago. I'm a woman – a hardworking and strong woman – and I know how to take care of myself." And with that, she pivots on her feet and walks away from me, leaving behind a distinct imprint of her painful words that etches itself onto the constricted confines of my chest.

6.
nia

Fuck him. Fuck him for getting such a reaction out of me, for making me feel things I told myself I wouldn't, not after how carelessly he broke my heart. Fuck him for making me question everything, most of all my sanity, just for the sake of his temporary presence in this town. I told him I'm not the same stupid girl from all those years ago, and I mean it. Then why am I acting like her right now? This is ridiculous. It's all just complete bullshit.

I huff against the brutal cold around me as I open my fence's door, but stop mid-step when I realize there is someone behind me. Slowly, with my heart pounding a mile a second, I turn and look towards the end of the street. My gut tightens when I see Cass, leaning casually against a black SUV, with his hands in his jeans pockets and long, errant strands of his hair flowing with the wind, looking at me with an expression that could only be labelled as longing.

Why? I want to scream at him, but don't have the strength to. Brandon's words from earlier are still nagging at me, and despite feeling weighed down by them, I can't stop thinking about the way Cass stood up for me, and the things he told me after.

And the words I practically spat at him before walking away from him.

I had been *this* close to telling him that I didn't need him – not after everything I've been through already. But… but it felt so *good* to have someone stand up for me like that. My family and friends have given my asshole of an ex-husband an ample amount of shit for treating me the way he has, but…but the way Cass silenced him, punched him in the *face* for badmouthing me…

Fuck me, that was hot. Him having such a strong reaction even after so many years – it lit something inside me. Brought something in me back to life, in a way.

I shake my head and look at him again. "Were you seriously following me?" I ask the obvious. Thank God for the cover of the night, otherwise he'd notice how flushed I am right now. Not because of the cold, but from seeing him look so effortlessly beautiful under the glaring moonlight.

"You don't live with your parents anymore," he says, then starts walking towards me.

I don't know why, but I step back, and back, and back until my ass hits the house door. "I was married, remember?"

"So?" He lifts a brow as he walks through the gate. "You're not married anymore." He climbs the one step that separates us, then gives me a crooked smile. "Déjà vu, huh?" he quips as he glances around my porch.

"I didn't wanna bother Mom and Dad after the divorce by staying with them, so I decided to get a place of my own. This house luckily went up for sale a week after I signed the divorce papers." I lift a shoulder. "Noah lives next door, and the café is only a few minutes from here. It's convenient and cozy."

Cass steps into my personal space, so I press my back further against the door. "I'm sorry about the whole Brandon thing," he whispers. "He…he was treating you like shit, Nia, and I can't even *imagine* the way he must've behaved with you during–"

"It's fine," I cut him off. "I dealt with it when I had to."

"But did you *really* have to?" he asks, then scans my face. "Did you?" He places a hand on the wall next to the side of my head, then leans in so close that I can see every speck of gold in his brown eyes.

"Cass…" I'm breathless, scared. I'm eager, frustrated.

"I'm not going to be *that guy* and say that I should've been there for you, and I'm not going to tell you that if I knew about the Brandon situation, I would've come running to bail you out of it. Because I seriously don't know what I would've done then, but it's like you said: you dealt with it when you had to. You're strong, Nia. So damn strong." He places his other hand next to the side of my face.

"You don't know me," I tell him. "You don't know me at all, Cass. You've *never* known me."

His expression hardens a little. "You know that's a lie."

"Do I?"

He steps closer still, resulting in us sharing a breath. "It *killed* me to leave–"

"Don't you dare bullshit me," I hiss.

"I'm not," he hisses back, then grits his teeth and brings his left hand between us before pushing back the sleeve of his sweater. "Look at this." He gestures at it. "*Look*."

I release a puff of air and do as he's asked. When my gaze lands on his wrist, I can't help but suck in a breath.

"It's *you*, Nia," Cass says with a strain in his voice. "You've always been with me, even when you thought I'd moved on. It's you; it's always been you."

I stare at my name – inked in black – written in simple yet stunning calligraphy on the inside of his wrist.

Nia

"You're the very pulse that helps me stay alive," he tells me. "You're the very beat my body obeys to, that it reacts to. I've had this tattoo for 6 years now. I got it done just so I could remind myself of what, and *who*, I left behind, but could never forget." He drops his arm by his side.

I'm at a loss for words, and he, of course, notices that.

He glances at my mouth, which does absolutely nothing to calm my already hay-wired senses.

"Kiss me, Nia."

"What?" In the midst of my trance, I do manage to ask a logical question. Not that it matters much, though, as I feel completely flustered under his gaze. But Jesus, he's *beautiful* when he demands something, so how the hell am I supposed to keep it together right now?

He shifts on his feet, and his belt buckle presses against my stomach. "*Kiss me*, Nia," he repeats, but this time in a voice that causes a shiver to run through my body.

"Cass, no." I shake my head. "We can't."

"Why not?" he asks so simply that it makes me blink.

"Because you left, dammit!" I yell. "You left, and I was here feeling hollow and devastated and…and *foolish*. I was a joke to everyone at school: a pathetic girl with dreams too big for her cloudy little head." I bite the inside of my cheek to stop my chin from trembling. "It broke me even more, their words of mockery. A tattoo doesn't fix everything you ruined for me. I just…" I sniff and run my fingers through my hair. "I…I can't."

"I'm here now," he says. "You know why I left, but I'm here now."

"But for how long, Cass?" I scoff. "You're here only to film a documentary. And what happens when you're done with that? What happens when you've gotten what you came for? I know what'll happen: you'll leave – just like you did before."

"Do you want me to apologize for it?" he sneers. "Do you want me to beg for your forgiveness for wanting to make a life out of myself? To *do* and *be* something in life? Is that what you want from me?"

"I don't want anything from you." I swallow and raise my hands in front of me, but clench them into fists and let them fall at my sides with another shake of my head.

"Touch me, Nia," Cass urges. "Push me, slap me, kick me, but touch me. Do something – *anything*, dammit. Just fucking touch me, because I'm going out of my mind here." He bends, and his nose to brushes mine. "Please."

"No…" I'm surprised my voice hasn't given up on me yet, despite the pressure in my throat.

Cass's eyes darken. "Fuck it, then." He erases the sorry excuse of a space between us and practically crashes his lips to mine.

I gasp, and he uses that as a chance to run his tongue over the roof of my mouth. He tastes like beer and mint, and maybe even cigarette. It's hard to keep track of everything, let alone commonsense, as he presses his hips against my navel and sucks on my bottom lip. His stubble scratches roughly against my skin as my lips move with his, making it burn insistently. I can't even compare his older kisses to what he's doing to me now, because it just wouldn't be fair. Those kisses were mild, maybe even a little shy. But this – this is possession. The way he parts my lips and takes what he wants – it's all-consuming. The way he moans into my mouth and presses his teeth into my bottom lip – it's inebriating.

I place my hands on his chest and make a vain attempt of pushing him away. "Cass, please, no–"

"Just shut up," he grunts, then starts kissing me again. His mouth drags hurriedly over my jaw, my neck, and my throat in fleeting bites, and I can't help but arch against him. His breaths fanning my skin are making me wet, and the weight of his hard body over mine is making me ache for him in a way I never have before.

"Cass…"

He groans as he licks a path from my throat to my chin, and when I part my lips for him, he devours me, taking every single one of my breaths for himself.

I claw at his jaw as I push my mouth harder against him, but he grabs my wrists, moves back, and grins down at me.

"If only you could look at yourself right now," he says to me. "Fuck, baby, you're a *marvel*." His gaze dips lower as he lets go of my wrists.

I'm panting as I wait for him to do something. His eyes gleam as he claims my mouth in another kiss, then touches the tips of his cold fingers to my chest, right before pushing down the front of my dress enough to expose my breasts.

I inhale a shocked breath and try to pull his hand away. "What are you–"

"Shh." He smirks, and when I try to speak again, he takes my right nipple into his mouth, making me moan out loud.

"*Fuck!*" My back bows off the door when the warmth of his mouth replaces the chill around us, causing goosebumps to prick my skin.

Cass bites my nipple – so hard that my vision turns spotty. His free hand cups and kneads my other breast, and he then starts alternating between sucking, pinching, and biting them both.

I know I'm going to have bruises all over, but as his lips once again wrap around my pebbled peaks and tug, I lose even the most basic train of thought.

Cass lets go of my nipple with a pop, then gives me a chaste kiss before stepping away from me. "Glad to know I've still got what it takes to make you tick." He winks at me, then lets out a yawn that can only be classified as fake.

"Forgive me, but I've had quite the day – you know, from traveling seven hours to get here, to punching your ex-husband, to making you so wet that I could practically smell you while getting a taste of your inviting tits." He scratches his stubble. "I think I'm gonna go and get some sleep now. But not before I jerk off to the sound of your voice when you moan for me, and your enticing body, of course." He back-walks until he's reached the SUV, then gives me a two-finger salute. "Goodnight, Nia." And with that, he gets in the car and drives off.

A chilling breeze hits me like a slap in the face, so I quickly fix my dress before slumping in front of my door. I bring my knees up, then place my elbows on top of them so that I can hold my head between my hands.

What the fuck just happened? I ask myself, then sigh and close my eyes when a beautiful chorus of redpolls singing on a nearby tree meets my ears, all but pleading with me to push aside my thoughts, if only for a while.

And so, I do, letting my doubts and reluctance drift away with the wind as I get lost in a song I don't really know the words to.

7.
cass

"We rolling yet?" I ask as I fix my hair.

"Yup," the cameraman answers, most definitely annoyed with me.

I raise my arms by my sides. "Come, now; don't be like that. I need to look presentable, alright?" I tell him. "The bun's gotta be on point and shit."

He rolls his eyes. "Got it."

I chuckle, then gesture at him to give me the cue.

He raises an arm and does the 3 count, then brings it down, and I immediately fall into work mode.

"You guys ever wonder how much school changes one's life?" I say into the camera, then smile. "My years at *Adenbrooke High* were most definitely fun and exciting, and filled with quite a few uncalled-for detentions that I didn't really care to attend." I lift a shoulder, just as Amanda and some of the crew laugh indulgently. "But hey, I did deem it fit to go to a few of 'em. I just made sure to drag some of my friends along with me." I point a thumb over my shoulder. "You guys ready to see the place that was my initial temple of mischief?"

The school grounds have been booked by the producers for filming, so the crew and I have the entire place to ourselves. It's perfect for giving the audience an undisturbed tour without running into students or the faculty. And I know that not everything we film is going to make the final cut, but at least this way, I get to revisit familiar grounds and relive some beautiful memories.

Three hours, and many, *many* rounds of the school premises later, we stop in front of what used to be my locker.

I grin and run my fingers over the fresh paint, and the sparkly stickers taped next to a few Andrew Garfield photos. Whoever is using my locker now has made sure to design it aesthetically, and as I step away from it, I feel the cameras zooming in on me.

"This locker," I begin, then glance at the lenses surrounding me, "is where I first realized that I was in love with my best friend." I chuckle. "She was just here – like she used to be every damn day – and we were talking about some random assignment when I… I looked at her and just *knew* that I was madly in love with her." Images of a flushed and bubbly 16-year-old Nia flash across my mind, and I swallow. She's always been a beacon of light in my life, and whenever I saw her during those days, I craved more of her; more of what she had to offer by just being herself.

I've always been drawn to her like a compass to the right direction, and even though we've grown up now, I still feel like that silly kid who'd fluster over her and touch her every chance he got.

I sigh and scratch my left forearm as I step further away from the locker. I haven't seen Nia since our little encounter outside her house 5 days ago. I don't have her number, and visiting her café or her house seems a bit excessive. The latter has crossed my mind more times than I can count, but I'm not sure if she'd be okay with it.

I've fucked my hand one too many times thinking about her these last few days, but dammit, I need more. I feel dizzy just by thinking about getting to feel her skin against mine again, and to have her breaths stuttering for me when I touch her once more. And I know I'm working, but my dick doesn't get the memo. A slight mention of Nia, and now I'm shamelessly hard behind my suffocating pair of stupid jeans.

"Cass?"

I turn, and smile when Amanda walks over to me. "Hey."

"Taking a mental trip down memory lane, huh?" she asks with a knowing look on her face.

I chuckle. "Kinda, yeah."

She touches my arm. "Me and a few of the producers are going to the nearest diner for breakfast. Come, join us."

I rub my jaw as thoughts of Nia once again fill my mind. "How about a raincheck?"

Something flashes across Amanda's features – something I can't put a finger on – but she gives me a nod and moves away with a smile I know to be mostly forced. "I'll see you at the B&B for the after-lunch shoot, then," she says.

I give her a nod, a bit confused by her sudden change of behavior. "For sure."

With another quick nod, she pivots on her heels and marches away.

I shake my head a little, wave at the crew who are wrapping things up in the corridor, then walk out of the hall and head towards the parking lot.

Remember how I mentioned not wanting to be excessive? Yeah, fuck that; I'm about to go be excessive as shit.

8.
nia

I scratch the back of my thigh and yawn out loud like a cat ready for her life-renunciation. I then pull my lavender silk shorts down from between my legs, and when the doorbell rings for what could very easily be the 9th time, I scowl and yell, "COMING!"

With the heater running in the living room, the temperature in the house is warm and inviting, which helps dissipate some of my annoyance towards whoever it is that decided to ring my doorbell today. Small mercies and all.

My alarm went off an hour ago, but because I'm an avid sleep-lover, I didn't feel like leaving my bed and going to the shop today. And also because I'm exhausted from all the extra hours Noah and I have had to put in because of the increasing demand of coffee due to the weather here.

I unlock the door before opening it, and almost close it back again when I see Cass leaning against the wall to his right. With his dark jeans, blue crewneck sweater, and black leather boots, along with his piercing gaze and that effortless man-bun of his, he looks just as put together as I look disheveled.

As I shift on my feet and hope to God that he isn't getting a first-hand whiff of my unwashed hair and damp armpits, he gives me a lazy once-over, then breaks into an amused grin when our eyes meet.

"Why do I always find you leaning against walls?" I ask him, just so things don't get awkward the longer we stand and stare at each other. "Is this a style thing, or have you developed a hip problem or something?"

He puts his tongue to his cheek and narrows his eyes at me. "If I tell you it's both, what then?"

"I'll pity you, of course. But then I'll shrug and shut the door in your face."

"But why haven't you shut the door on me already?"

"I'm waiting for you to tell me why you're here," I say. "And once you do, you'll have itched my curiosity, and I'll have the perfect prompt to close the door on you."

"Wow; good morning to you, too," he deadpans as he steps forward, then glances at my head. "I see we're favoring the crow's nest today," he adds, making my nostrils flare.

"You—" I barely get a word out before he wraps his calloused fingers around my throat and takes my mouth in an unrelenting kiss.

I fist his sweater and try to push him back, but he grabs my ass in a painful grip and continues to fuck my mouth.

"Mmm…" I don't realize it's *me* who made that sound until Cass smiles against my lips and kisses me faster, harder.

"Have you been fucked in the ass, Nia?" he asks, his voice like sandpaper. He traces my face with gleaming, all-showing eyes. "Have you?"

I'm out of breath as I answer him. "That's none of your business."

"I know, but I want it to be," he says easily.

I just…stare at him in incredulity.

"Are you being serious right now?" I sneer before moving out of his hold. "Do you really think it's that easy, Cass? Do you think I'm going to let you in and ruin me all over again? Do you really think I'm that…gullible that I'll let you take away my newfound normalcy from me?" I push back my hair and try not to look him in the eyes when his expression turns from lustful to hurtful.

"I just…I don't get what you're trying to achieve here," I admit. "You follow me home after returning to town, kiss me on my porch and leave me shocked and confused, then come back here days later to do exactly that, hoping I'll give in completely this time. And for what – to get a rebound before you leave for good? To know that you've still got what it takes to fool me? Is that what it is for you?"

"Nia." He tries to touch me, but I jerk away from him. "You're making it harder than it should be."

"Am I?" I glare at him. I'm so pissed at myself for letting him get to me again. So fucking disappointed.

Cass's jaw hardens. "You *are*." He steps into the house and shuts the door with a *bang*. "Why is it so goddamn difficult for you? Why does everything with you have to be so dramatic and complicated?"

"*Me?*" I sneer at him. "Look who's talking. Complicated should be *your* second name." I point a finger at him. "You don't know what the fuck you want. You don't know how hard it is for me. You don't know how I wasted *months* of my life pining for you – praying you'd come back. You. Don't. Know. *Anything*."

He has the audacity of looking surprised. "Do you seriously think I'm that dense? Do you honestly think I felt – *feel* – nothing?"

I clench my hands and grit my teeth. "Leave."

"No." He walks closer to me.

I stand my ground and look up at him. "*Leave*, Cass."

His chest rises and falls unsteadily. "And what if I don't?"

I'm angry. So *fucking* angry.

Angry at the easy question I'm incapable of answering.

At the vulnerability on his face.

At the desire I feel so deep in my gut that it's hard not to let it cloud my thoughts.

I turn and head for my bedroom, because really, I need to create as much distance between us as I can, but he grabs my hand and pulls me to him, making me stumble against his hard frame.

"Don't walk away from me again," he whispers. "Don't do what you did all those years ago."

"You don't have the right to–"

"Leaving you behind was *torturous*, Nia, can't you fucking understand that? I had no choice. I wanted *more*, and for that, I sacrificed you. I sacrificed everything you and I had. But I don't regret it, and if this – this moment we're sharing – is my chance to fix what I so selfishly let go, then I'll take it; I'll try my best to make it okay."

"You don't deserve it." I shove him away. "You don't deserve a second chance, a new path, or even a single moment. You don't deserve anything. You don't deserve *me*."

"I like to think that I do. Everyone deserves a new page, a fresh start."

"But what's the point of it if you're just going to leave that chapter incomplete and bail out of the chance I give you?" I yell. "What then, huh? What happens then?"

He swallows. "Why don't you try me; give me a fair shot."

I can't help the crude laugh that leaves me. "I don't trust you."

"You don't have to trust me to put me to the test," he counters. "What we had, Nia, isn't something that just goes away. If anything, it ages with time and becomes stronger. Don't you feel what I'm feeling right now – that pull, that raw need to taste, to consume, and to earn?"

Goosebumps prick my scalp at his words. My nipples harden; my pussy throbs. The effect he has on me is insane, but is it even valid anymore?

Do I even care if it isn't?

I shake myself out of the absurd idea. Of course I care. He left me once, and I wouldn't put it past him to do it again.

"You should go," I tell him. "Please, just…just go, Cass. I cannot and will not do this to myself a second time."

"Why are you so scared?" he questions. "Why are you so fucking hesitant? You're single; I'm single. We can at least try things again, baby."

"Don't call me that," I spit out.

I see anger – clear and hot – on his face. "Only if you tell me you don't want me."

"Fuck you." I swallow the lump in my throat and sniff against the burning in my nose.

"Well, I'm not leaving until I know for sure what you want, Nia," he pushes.

I clench my jaw as I glare at him, but my anger once again fails to shield me from him when he looks down at me with pure admiration in his eyes.

My breath hiccups in my throat; I really don't know what to do or say right now.

Cass notices it, of course. And so, with his gaze fixed on me, he inclines his head in my direction. "Take off your clothes," he commands.

I blink. "What?" The word is barely a whisper as it slips past my lips.

"Your clothes – take 'em off," he states. "Either that, or ask me to leave. Anything, Nia. Give me *anything*."

I swallow again, but this time, it feels as though thorns have clawed their way up to my throat. And then I say something that I'm pretty sure I didn't intend to say out loud. Oh well.

"I want *you* to take off your clothes first."

Cass's brows furrow for a brief moment, but then a sinister sort of look takes over his face. He clutches the hem of his sweater, then pulls the soft fabric up and over his head before letting it fall to the floor.

My mouth quite literally dries out as I look at his smooth skin, at his lean waist and his cut-to-precision abs. At the V of his hips and the patch of dark hair behind the waistband of his jeans.

I watch, spellbound, as he unbuckles his belt and throws it to the side. I can't move. My body has lost its ability to function. Watching Cass as he undresses himself is the only thing I can think of doing.

He unbuttons his jeans, and when he pushes both it and his underwear down before getting to his full height, my pussy clenches as I see his cock.

"Fuck me," I all but breathe the words as I stare at the curved barbell with two large, silver beads on each end, pierced on the underside of Cass's jutted length.
"Oh my…" I shift a little. "Umm…wow."

He laughs. "Weren't expecting this, were you?"

I shake my head. "No…" I bite my lower lip. "And I'm not going to act shallow and ask if it hurt, because I know for sure that it must have. But…can I ask why, though? I didn't think you were into something like this."

Cass starts walking towards me, at complete ease with his nudity.

My gaze momentarily lands on the piercing again, and then on his face.

"An impulsive decision, made after a few glasses of whiskey and a raunchy threesome," he confesses.

Questionable rage and jealousy flare through me. "I see."

He cants his head to the side. "You don't like it?" he asks.

"Don't like what?"

"The piercing, Nia," he states coolly.

"It's not the piercing I mind; it's the reason behind it," I tell him honestly.

"I was 20, babe. Horny and high-on-the-feeling. I felt like I could conquer it all, and I frankly didn–"

"Please don't justify anything." I lift a shoulder. "You don't have to."

"Why are you being so fucking impossible?" he hisses.

I get in his face. "Am I?"

He fists my hair and pulls, resulting in a delicious kind of pain to zap through my scalp. "It's a good thing I'm mad for you, otherwise I'd have shoved my cock so deep down your throat that you'd have no other choice but to shut the hell up."

"*Fuck you*."

"Oh, you will, but not before I've gotten a taste of you." He crashes his mouth to mine, and as I close my eyes, he moves his hand from my hair and hastily pulls me flush against his body. "You look hot in a camisole and shorts, but they've gotta go," he growls.

I gasp when he practically hauls my clothes off me, and as I kick them away, he lifts me up and places my back against the door.

"Damn-fucking-it." He looks at me with a crazed desire on his face, then starts trailing bruising kisses from my neck, all the way down to my chest. Every touch of his lips and scrape of his stubble on my skin is an imprint of promise – of what he can do to me and my weak lucidity.

He sets me down, then gets down on his knees in front of me. "Take a step forward," he says.

I do.

"Widen your legs."

Again, I do as I'm told.

"Good." He runs the tip of his tongue over his bottom lip, then spread my pussy with his fingers before grinning up at me. "You still don't shave often, huh?"

I shrug. "You know I don't like it."

His grin broadens. "I love it that you don't like it." He flicks my clit, and I cry out.

"More," I moan.

Cass chuckles. "You got it." He bends and sucks on my folds, then takes my clit in his mouth, and I almost lose my balance with the way that makes me feel.

"Spread your legs wider," he orders in between licks.

I open myself up further.

He cups my ass and squeezes, and then shifts forward, which gives him better access to me.

"Cass…" I bunch his hair in a fist and rock my hips in time with his tongue. "Ah, *fuck*. Cass…"

"Mm." He lets go of my clit, then starts eating me out faster. "Ride my face, Nia," he says. "Ride my face like the good fucking girl I know you are."

With a groan that is very unlike me, I start rocking against Cass's mouth as he continues to lick and suck my sensitive pussy.

I can feel myself falling over; feel myself getting to the pinnacle I know will give me the orgasm that I'm craving so fucking badly. But…but I don't want this to end, not until he's inside me again.

"Cass." I tug at his hair. "Cass, stop."

He looks up at me. "You okay?"

"Yes, of course." I let go of a breath. "It's just… It's hot; *you're* hot. And everything inside me is just…"

"Too heightened to control?" he completes.

"Yeah." I chuckle. "Fucking *yes*."

Cass gets to his feet. "I know what you mean," he says, then runs a knuckle over my painfully hard nipple.

I slowly drag a finger over his treasure trail as I lower my gaze, and relish the feeling of his abs tightening in response.

"I could never even compare to you," I say absentmindedly. "You're…you're *beautiful*, Cass."

He cups my face and bends to look into my eyes. "You can't, but that's only because you're already ranked way above me."

My heart beats rapidly at that. "Flawed compliments will take you nowhere."

He grins. "Well, it's a good thing I'm an honest guy, then."

I chuckle around a shake of my head, then tilt my head to the side. "Touch yourself," I tell him.

If he's shocked by my command, he doesn't show it. He simply smirks and fists his cock, and I see my name on the inside of his wrist moving with every single pump of his hand.

"Fuck." His Adam's apple bobs as he strokes himself. "Jesus Christ." He works himself more, and I watch as a thick bead of precum slides down from his slit and onto his piercing. "Nia…" He slows his pace, then places a hand on the wall next to my face before leaning close to me. "I love how you taste on my tongue," he says, then bends to suck on the skin beneath my ear, making me moan. "Mm, you smell so good, baby." He grazes his lips over the shell of my ear. "So good."

I spread my legs further and cup the nape of his neck. "Fuck me, Cass," I order.

He moves back and scans my face. "You sure?" he asks.

I nod. "And before you ask: yes, I'm clean, and no, we don't need a condom. I'm on a pill."

He grins. "So eager…" He rubs his crown over my clit. "Oh, and by the way, I'm clean too."

"*Lovely*." I bunch his soft hair in a rough grip. "Now, put that cock inside me and fuck my pussy, because I'm quite literally losing my mind right now."

He lets go of a surprised laugh. "Aye, ma'am." He lifts me up, and as I wrap my legs around his waist, he rocks his hips forward and enters me in a single thrust.

I hiss as he stretches me, and when the cold steel of his piercing meets my skin, I clench around him in a silent request for him to give me more.

He grabs my waist and pushes forward, burying himself deep inside me.

"God, *yes*," I breathe, pulling his mouth to mine.

"Feels good, huh?" he says, thrusting into my harder.

"More than," I reply, just as breathless as him.

He moans against my lips before kissing me, then rotates his hips and pushes into me with abandon.

I groan and tighten my hold on his hair because *God*, that piercing of his is driving me mad in the most delicious way possible.

He grunts and pushes into me deeper. "That's right; clench that cunt 'round my cock," he hisses. "Fucking clench it, baby."

I hum and do what he wants me to, which makes him grin.

Is this what complete, utter bliss looks like? Is this how it feels to be entirely unhooked from reality, to be lost in something – *someone* – who worships you for who you are?

Is it safe for me? For him?

For our hearts?

The sounds of our heavy, uneven breathing, and of our thighs slapping against each other's as Cass fucks me, are the only things I can hear as my ears buzz and warmth fills my belly.

I place my left hand on his heaving chest. "Faster, Cass," I whisper, and curse when he delivers. My back arches off the door, and sweat trickles down my temples as my orgasm washes over me in a blinding wave.

"Shit," he spits out, and starts moving inside me a bit unsteadily.

I massage the back of his head, and watch as his lashes shadow his cheeks when he closes his eyes. He bunches his jaw and touches his forehead to mine, and with one last thrust, he calls my name before coming inside me.

I can feel, and hear my pulse as I try to catch my breath. I run the pads of my fingers over his abs, and he nuzzles his nose against mine.

"So…" He lets the word hang in the air.

I chuckle and kiss his sweat-slicked lips. "So…"

He smiles, and our eyes meet. "You've officially left me crazed once again, Nia Connell," he says.

My throat tightens at his words. "And you, Cass Madden, have officially left me craving for more, just like before."

"Hmm, I kinda like the sound of that," he muses, then slowly pulls out of me. "Let me help you clean up."

And there goes my heart, fluttering helplessly with the wind.

"Okay." I wrap my arms around his neck and kiss him again. "Thank you."

"What for?" he asks.

I shrug. "For being you, I guess."

He grins. "Well, in that case, thank you to you, too."

I arch a brow in question.

He searches my face while holding onto me tighter. "For giving me a second chance," he tells me.

And as I struggle to find the right words to say to him, I keep looking at the candidly beautiful man in front of me – who has made me feel alive again after years of staying shadowed by my fear of disappointing those I care about.

I've always lived my life for others. Never for myself, but only for those around me. With Cass, though, it feels like I'm living for *me*. Like I'm breathing and laughing and smiling for *myself*.

Fuck, I'm falling irreversibly in love with this man for the second time around, aren't I?

Why yes; yes, I am.

9.
cass

I'm a complete goner for this woman. I'm drowning in her; I'm falling too hard, too fast for her. It's a feeling I'm familiar with, yet it feels amazingly foreign this time.

Every moan I've elicited from her, every kiss we've shared, every request of hers that I've fulfilled – it keeps replaying in my head on a loop. Because I can't, for the life of me, stop thinking about any of it.

Being with her is like crashing against a current that is bound to reach the shore. She keeps me adrift with her smile, with her touch. She makes me feel whole with her kisses, with her laughter. With eyes that speak volumes, and a voice that calms the ones in my head, she makes me feel like myself again. And that, for me, is eternal bliss – one I consider myself lucky to be subjected to.

10.
cass

"Hey, guys." I wave at my phone's camera, then turn to show the viewers the open space behind the B&B, capped beautifully in thick sheets of snow. "It's another day of filming the documentary. We've yet to set things up for the day, so while I wait for the crew to get on with it, I thought I'd show you all the gorgeous view I'm currently witnessing." A gust of cold wind whips by me, making me shiver. "Jesus," I mutter, then chuckle. "I'd forgotten how relentlessly chilly Adenbrooke can get during the winters," I say, then brush the snow off my hair and stubble. "Oh, and I'm sorry for not posting as much on my YouTube channel, and on here as well. I know you guys like my reels, but with filming and trying to stay in shape without a gym, I've hardly had time to create content for y'all. But I promise that once I'm back in NYC, I'll be posting as much as I can. So, stay tuned, and I'll keep updating you guys on the documentary's progress. Peace." I hit post on my IG stories, and scowl when the upload buffer moves at the pace of a sexually frustrated sloth.

"Hey." Her voice sounds from behind me, right before I feel her presence on my back.

I grin before turning around to face her, and there she is, dressed from head to toe in fuzzy wool and denim.

"You're *really* feeling it today, aren't you?" I tell her.

"My *hair* is frozen," she mutters. "Like, *all of it*."

I laugh, then gesture at the white cups she's holding. "What's this?"

Nia hands one of them to me, then sniffs and rubs a hand over her face. "Hot cocoa." She shudders a little, so I quickly move forward and wrap an arm around her.

"Nice…but I'd rather drink *you*," I tell her.

She scrunches up her nose. "You know I can punch you right in the jugular for making that ridiculous comment, don't you?"

"I play with fire for a reason, baby."

"Oh my God, get your face out of my *sight*," she mumbles.

I raise a brow. "I'm sorry, but are you *complaining*?" When she doesn't answer me, and instead narrows her eyes at me in silent disapproval, I decide to push her a little, simply to get a reaction out of her. I gotta keep up with my reputation of being an absolute fiend, after all.

"Well, I didn't hear you complaining yesterday when I was fucking you in the bar's storeroom," I tell her.

She sucks in a breath, and a blush begins creeping up her cheeks.

I smirk and pull her flush against me. "You liked it, didn't you, Nia?" I glance at her mouth, and her lips part as she exhales while looking up at me.

"You liked it when the racked beer bottles rattled with each thrust of my hips, didn't you?" I continue. "You liked it when I made you come so hard you could barely walk for the next hour. You liked it when my cock pushed in and out of your tight little cunt and made you whimper. And you most definitely liked it when I tightened my fingers around your throat and stroked you until you came all over my hand. You did, didn't you, baby?"

It's been a week since I asked Nia to give me a second chance. A week since she gave it to me. A week of maddening kisses and endless sex; of stolen winks and suggestive smiles. I've quite literally been in heaven, and as my team gets done with some candid shots of the town before the final few days of filming, I can't wait to see what the next chapter for Nia and I will be.

I have to admit, though: I'm *terrified* of what her decision will be regarding us, but I'm confident that she'll make a choice she thinks is right for *her*. She knows my stay in Adenbrooke is coming to an end, and I appreciate that she's willing to keep herself and I a priority, even with her life in the town and *Café Connell* both working in tangent with each other. And I may be selfish when it comes to her, but I can't force her to do something I know she wouldn't want to. I'll try, I'll fight, but not at the expense of her comfort and happiness. I know when to give up, but right now – with how things are – I'm just going to sit back and greedily accept every second she chooses to spend with me. One step at a time, as they say.

"Cass!"

I turn at the sound of Amanda's voice, and watch as she trudges over to me, kicking and cursing at the snow that is covering her boots.

Nia, flustered and shocked, stumbles away from me.

"Hey," I greet my manager with a grin.

Amanda eyes me and Nia for a beat too long – her expression hard under the dull morning light – then cracks a smile that had made me wanna piss my pants when I'd first met her 6 years ago.

When my YouTube career skyrocketed in 2015, a fellow influencer suggested I get in touch with Amanda for professional management services. I gotta say: as a 21-year-old who had no idea what to do with the newfound fame and attention I was receiving on my content, I was relieved to have someone to guide me through the ins and outs of the media world, but my initial meeting with Amanda had felt more like a one-on-one with a school principal than anything else. That woman is dangerously cunning, and will take no bullshit from anyone, and I mean *anyone*. Not even from me and my occasionally whiny ass, if I'm being honest.

"I'm afraid we haven't…met?" she says to Nia, then folds her arms across her chest.

Nia, who looks like she'll plummet face-first onto the ground if my manager so much as *tries* to move in her direction, fidgets with the purple scarf around her neck as she shifts on her feet. "Yeah, uh… I, umm–"

"Amanda, this is Nia," I say. "And Nia," I jerk my chin ahead, "that's Amanda, my manager." I then take a long gulp of my hot cocoa, because *damn*, the air around us just got real thick.

Amanda quickly glances at my left wrist, and even though it's currently hidden behind the sleeve of my sweater, I know she recalls the name from my tattoo.

She nods, then smiles curtly. "Right. Of course. Nia, yes; that's correct."

Nia looks like she wants a UFO to fly by and pull her up with the way she's trying to squirm at the awkwardness of the whole…*situation*.

Amanda has that effect on everyone, I want to tell her, but don't. What I instead do is save us all from the general embarrassment that keeps growing due to the lack of interest either of the women are showing in conversing with each other by clearing my throat and wrapping an arm around Nia once again. Amanda, of course, tracks that movement with apt interest, but doesn't say anything.

"You wanna get outta here?" I ask Nia, as softly as I can.

She visibly relaxes under my touch as she looks at me. "Please, and thank you."

I bite the inside of my cheek to stop myself from laughing. "Let me show you my room, then; come on." I remove my arm from around her shoulders and grab her hand, and have only just started walking us towards the B&B when Amanda calls out my name, stopping me.

"Yes, Miss Manager?" I muse as I shift slightly to glance at her.

Something like anger crosses her features. "Filming starts in a few minutes."

I gesture around us. "I see no setup."

"I have ordered for things to be up and running in a bit."

"Well, then call for me when they are *up and running*."

Her jaw ticks as she glares at me. "I think you should stay here."

I let go of Nia's hand and turn, completely put-off by Amanda's insistence. "I think I'll go up to my room and spend some time with Nia until things are ready here."

Nia touches my arm. "Hey, it's okay, Cass. I'll come by later."

"I think that's a good id–" Amanda starts, but I cut her off.

"You're not going anywhere," I tell Nia.

Both women stare at me, and I can hear even the smallest hiss of the wind with how quiet things have gotten.

Nia squeezes my bicep in a silent request to let this go. "Cass, it's fine, really; I'll just–"

"I think we've gotten off on the wrong foot here," I tell them. "We gotta re-evaluate and shit, don't you agree?" When neither of them answers, I scrub a hand over my stubble. "How about we go to dinner together – tomorrow. Just the 3 of us. Have a sit-down, get candid, grab a few drinks. What do you think?"

Nia makes a noise that I assume stands for a yes, whereas Amanda squares her shoulders and inclines her head a little.

I flash her a winning smile. "Great; that's settled, then." I once again grab Nia's hand, which is a little clammy this time around, and tell her, "Let's go see my room, babe."

11.
cass

Nia chugs the last of her hot cocoa and throws her cup into the trashcan in my bedroom. "*What the fuck just happened?*" she asks incredulously.

I throw my empty cup in the bin and turn on the heater. "Your guess is as good as mine."

She rakes her fingers through her hair half-frozen hair. "She's just so…just so…"

"Frustratingly wicked?" I provide.

She lets her arms rise and fall by her sides. "*Ugh!*"

I chuckle as I move further into the room. "Relax; you'll get used to it. But if it's any consolation, I'll have you know that she's in a good mood today." I lift a shoulder.

Nia rolls her eyes. "Lucky me."

"She doesn't take to change easily," I tell her. "She has mostly always behaved this way towards women I've dated in the past. I guess it's her way of making sure I'm not being used for my popularity or status in the social media world; her way of eliminating the bad fish and all that."

Nia's expression turns distant, but she clears her throat and eases herself from it. She then looks around the wood-finished room and furniture, the unlit fireplace and shut glass window, and shakes her head at me. "I can't believe you made an excuse of wanting to show me your *room* to get us out of that nauseous situation. Like you and I haven't been inside this B&B countless times during dozens of fairs and events as kids."

"I had to use some sort of escape route, didn't I? Stuff wasn't necessarily getting any mellow between the two of you."

Nia clicks her tongue. "She doesn't even know me, and yet she acted like she despises me. Like I spat in her coffee or something."

"You just *had* to reference coffee, didn't you?" I ask with a raise of my brow. "Did you really have to be that cliché?"

I can tell that she's fighting back a smile with the way she presses her lips together. "I'm not creative with words, okay? Have some mercy on me."

"Excuses, excuses."

She flips me off, and when I come to stand right in front of her, she slowly drags her eyes over my body. "The years have definitely worked wonders on you, haven't they?"

A surprised laugh leaves me at her words. "You noticed that *now*?"

She shrugs. "I've been observing it bit by bit during the last few days."

"Is that a compliment? Because I can't tell if it is."

"Just take what you can, Madden," she snarks. "And try not to fucking question it."

"Fair point," I agree. I then pull my phone out of my pocket and hit play on *Sentiments*, by Jenaux and Bryce Fox, before placing it on the nightstand next to us.

Nia arches a brow.

"I noticed that you like this song," I tell her simply.

She chuckles, then hooks a finger into the waistband of my jeans before tugging me towards her. "I do," she says, then gives me a quick kiss. "Cass?"

My cock hardens at the way she says my name, and my breaths stumble when I see a glimmer of mischief in her bright blue eyes. "Yeah?"

She presses another kiss on my lips, then lazily brushes the back of her fingers over my jaw. "Your hair – untie it," she orders.

I grin, then pull the hairband off my hair before tossing it on the bed.

Nia visibly sucks in a breath when my long hair falls forward, curtaining the sides of my face.

"You're this…outrageously sexier version of a Greek demigod or some shit," she says in a slight rush, which makes me laugh.

"I'm sorry, but are you mocking me?"

"What did I tell you about taking what you can get and not questioning it?"

I raise my hands in surrender. "Alright, alright; I give up."

"Good boy," she praises, then smiles before tugging at my waistband again. "Come here," she whispers, and takes my mouth in a demanding kiss.

With one hand on the side of her hip and the other on the wall behind her, I push myself against her and part my lips for her.

The song reaches its bridge, and Nia and I continue kissing each other like we're on borrowed time; like the very air we're breathing is toxic compared to the taste of each other.

I smile against her lips when she slips her hands under my sweater and drags her nails over my abs. "Nia…"

"Mmm." She moves them lower, and with a soft bite on my tongue, she unbuckles and unzips my jeans. When I grunt in approval, she slides a hand into my underwear and grabs the base of my hard cock.

"*Fuck*," I moan against her mouth. "Wrap your fingers around it tighter."

She moves back and meets my eyes, then squeezes me a little before fisting me slowly. "Like this?"

"Faster."

She obeys, and our breathing turns uneven as she continues stroking me.

She pulls at my piercing, twists it around, and then pulls at it again, which results in a dizzying wave of pleasure pain to shoot down to my balls.

"Jesus *Christ*," I hiss, then stumble against her body.

"I wanna feel your cum dripping down my fingers, Cass," she whispers in my ear.

"God, woman." I nuzzle my nose against the side of her neck, and inhale the smell of her honey-sweet perfume as I begin pumping my hips in time with her fist. "Dammit." I suck and bite on her soft skin, which makes her moan out loud.

My stomach clenches at her voice, and I continue to fuck her hand until…

Someone knocks on the door – no, they fucking *bang* on it.

I move back, dazed and more than annoyed, and whip my head towards it. "*What?*" I all but bark.

"Uh…sir – Cass…I…"

I clench my jaw and step away from Nia when she lets go of my cock. "What is it, Randall?"

He clears his throat. "Things have been set up on the grounds, sir – uh, Cass. Everyone is waiting for you outside."

I fix my jeans, buckle up my belt, and try not to lose my temper as I say, "Tell Amanda that I don't appreciate her indirect meddling, and that I'll meet her downstairs in a couple of minutes."

He's silent for a moment. "Umm… Should I really tell her the first bit?"

I pull open the door, and he all but stumbles at the suddenness of it.

"Did you hear me stuttering while I said those words, Randall?" I ask.

"…No?"

I lift a brow at him, to which he clears his throat and gives me a nod.

"I'll…go tell Amanda what you just said to me." He nods again – more to himself this time. "Yeah. I'll, uh, I'll go now." With an abrupt shift, he almost burns through the carpet as he runs away from me.

I close my eyes and place my forehead against the doorframe.

"Why did you have to be so hard on him?" comes Nia's voice, right before she rubs a hand on my back and presses a long kiss on my shoulder. "He's just doing his job, Cass; give him a break."

I turn and look at her. "I'm annoyed, okay? Give *me* a break."

"So, being annoyed automatically gives you the right to act like a bitch to him?" she retorts.

I snort. "I did *not* act like a bit–"

"You can try to justify that until the end of time, but I'll never agree with you," she challenges.

I chuckle, loosening up a bit. "How did I end up having such luck – to have someone in my life who doesn't even blink before calling me a bitch?"

She bats her lashes and gives me a clinical smile. "You may wanna ask Amanda about that. I'm sure she's transcribing an answer for that as we speak."

I grin and cup the back of her head before giving her a chaste kiss.

"Stop." She gives my chest a slight push. "You need to go now, Cass. The crew is waiting for you downstairs."

I step back. "Fine, but I'm coming over tonight."

"I know." She tangles and drags her fingers through my hair. "I'll go do stupid things until then in order to pass the time."

I wink at her. "*I'm* stupid, do *me*."

"*Ugh*." She pushes me away. "I can't believe you said that."

"Admit it, you secretly loved it."

She rolls her eyes. "I'm not going to give you the satisfaction of that in this lifetime, I assure you."

"Evil," I say around a grin.

She rises on her tiptoes and sets a soft kiss on the side of my mouth. "Mm-hmm. The best of her kind, don't you dare forget that."

12.
cass

With a shake of my head, I chuckle and rise on an elbow. "You're going to get all dizzy if you don't stop doing that," I tell her.

Nia, with a serene look on her face, continues spinning around the open, snow-laden field we're in. With her right hand in front of her chest, and the left one on top of her head, she turns, causing the flared hem of her blue velvet dress to brush against the powdered snow under us. Her long hair – wavier than usual – flows wildly with the strong afternoon wind, and when the muted daylight catches her at just the right moment, I sit up and continue looking at her because I've never seen anything more beautiful than her in my life so far. Watching Nia as she takes in the little pleasures of nature with such interest and calm is very soothing to be a part of.

She's like a silhouette, a mesmerizing portrait under the sky's unparalleled halo.

She finally stops spinning. With her back to me, she inhales, and then exhales slowly.

She had called me late last night and convinced me to attend Gerald's wedding with her. He's one of her regular customers at the café, and also a guy of eccentric tastes, if I do say so myself.

The church had been decorated with flowers of so many shapes, sizes, and colors that they'd not only given me a spotty vision by the end of the ceremony, but had also poked my sleeping pollen allergies. I don't think I've sneezed as much in the last ten years as I did in the hour I spent in the church listening to the 77-year-old Gerald reciting his vows to his now husband, Jasper. The two had met at *Café Connell*, and even though there's a 15-year age gap between them, it hasn't affected their chemistry or affection for each other.

Nia had been all smiles while seeing Jasper and Gerald tie the knot, and when I'd asked her to come to the field with me after the ceremony, she'd giddily said yes. Noah, of course, had given me his signature 'elder brother look' – one I've been a victim to numerous times in the past – to which I'd simply winked and given him a two-finger salute before driving Nia and I to the field.

After a long stretch of my neck, I fix my hair and get to my feet, then dust off my jeans before walking over to Nia.

"What're you thinking about?" I ask her as I wrap my arms around her waist. Moving her hair over one shoulder, I place my chin on the other, then press a kiss on the shell of her ear when she leans into me.

"My wedding," she answers, then sighs.

I stiffen a bit. "Yeah?"

"Yup." She sighs again. "I was just thinking about how everything on Bran and I's wedding day had felt: elementary and monotone. It was *nothing* compared to Gerald and Jasper's ceremony. Ours was…abrupt and suffocating. I guess

I knew things would be that way for him and I, but I went along with it anyway. I don't know what that says about me, but seeing Ger and Jas today made me realize how big of a mistake it was to marry Brandon; how I deserve to have something as beautiful as…" Her voice cracks a little, so she clears her throat. "I'm sorry, I shouldn't have said that."

"Hey." I turn her around, and when she looks at me, I cup her face between my hands. "Just stare into my eyes, Nia, and you'll *see*," is all I tell her. Because I know that she knows exactly what I'm talking about.

Our gazes meet, and I let her study me; I bare my truth to her in clear silence. And when she finds everything I want her to find, she lets go of a breath, and a tear slides down her cheek. "I–"

"I mean it," I whisper. "Everything you see, I mean it. Everything you know you just read on my face, I mean that, too. I know it'll be a long road for us, baby, but know that it'll be *ours* to hike; ours to conquer. I didn't ask you for another chance for nothing. I did it 'cause I intend to live up to it."

She grabs my wrists and gives them a squeeze. "That morning when you asked me for a second chance, I lied when I said I didn't trust you. I…" She sniffs. "The thing is: I trust you too much, but I don't trust myself at *all*. Around you, it's hard for me to. There's something about you that weakens my defenses. It never bothered me before, but now…" She shrugs.

I chuckle and press a kiss between her brows. "And you frustrate me to the point where I can't see straight. Your stubbornness is both hot and infuriating, but I like feeling the brunt of it." I bring my hands to her waist.

She laughs. "You really have a way with words, don't you?"

"I've been told I've got a talent for it, yes."

She snorts and gives my jaw a playful slap.

"So… You ready for dinner with Amanda tonight?" I ask.

Nia's expression hardens all of a sudden. "Can we not just cancel it?"

I tilt my head to it side. "And why would we do that?"

"Do you even have to ask?" She shifts on her feet. "That woman doesn't like me, Cass, and she made that *abundantly* clear yesterday with the way she looked at me – no, *judged* me."

"And that's exactly what I want to fix, Nia," I say. "I want to clear the air between you and her. The two of you are important to me, and I want to smooth out any misunderstanding or misjudgment yesterday's brief encounter might've caused."

"Cass–"

"3 years ago, when I first started working with actual celebrities on their fitness regime," I cut her off, "I…entered a phase where I decided that I had to live up to my name, to my newfound position." I scoff and shake my head. "This phase was short, sure, but it…it left me in a place that I don't ever wanna go back to. I've worked really hard to get out of it, and I'm never, *ever* going there again." I look at Nia, and see that the color has fully drained from her face.

"What…do you mean?"

"I…" I exhale and rub a hand over the back of my neck. "Well, let's just say that I overexerted myself. I wanted to be better than what – *who* – I was, and in doing so, I forgot that my body could only take so much. I erased boundaries; I ignored the warnings. I began resorting to certain…substances to help improve my physical appearance, and it's so damn crazy to think about it now, but at the time, I thought what I was doing was completely okay and necessary." I swallow when Nia places a hand over her mouth.

"You didn't–"

"No, but I got close," I admit. "The consequences of my recklessness quickly caught up to me. Lying in a hospital bed for weeks made me more and more miserable. At one point, I even started thinking about the permanent relief I would feel if I could just man up and pull the plug on–"

"Don't." Nia is crying as she shakes her head. "Don't fucking finish that sentence, or I swear to God I'll–"

"What, kill me?" I say.

She slaps me – so hard that it stings the entire left side of my face, and even makes my head throb in pain.

"Fuck you," she spits out.

"Sorry." I frown. "That was immature of me."

"You think?" She glares at me. "Do you have any idea what that confession just did to me?" She swallows and wipes a hand over her cheeks.

I lean in and touch my forehead to hers. "I'm sorry," I repeat. "I'm really, *really* sorry."

She tries to shove me away, but I grab her hands and kiss her knuckles to let her know that I really do feel guilty for my choice of words.

And for the things I did in the past.

"I just…I wanted you to know that when I was at my lowest, it was *Amanda* who pulled me out of it," I tell her. "It was her, Nia, who snapped me from it and made me see that I was enough; that it was *me* who the people wanted, and not some superficial version I was trying to create." I move back and wipe the fresh tears that have fallen down her face. "Amanda may be a difficult person to have an interaction with, but she does have a heart. She cares and understands. I just want you and her to give each other a chance, that's all."

"I could have lost you," Nia breathes with a look of horror on her face, then bunches her jaw when it trembles. "I could have lost you and I would have never even known." She closes her eyes. "I would have lived my entire fucking life not knowing what happened to you. Our past would have been the only thing – the only *memory* – I'd have of you, all because I–"

"Nia."

"Shut up." She pulls me to her and kisses me once, twice, and then a third time. "God, I could have lost you," she says again, then kisses me so hard I lose my ability to breathe for a moment.

"Baby…" I can taste tears on her lips as I kiss her back.

"If you ever think about doing something like that again, I'm going to kick your ass so fucking hard, Madden," she warns.

I bite the inside of my cheek. "And I promise that I'll let you."

She kisses me one more time. "I'm so happy you're here with me." She places a hand on my chest. "I'm so glad you had Amanda with you when you needed a solid support system."

"Yeah." I sigh. "Mom and Dad were completely broken when they found out, but they were there for me anyway – no questions or hesitation whatsoever. They are part of the reason I recovered so soon. They may not have shown, but I know how much my stupidity really affected them. Took them a little over a year to relax around me and not fuss over me like I was a wayward kid or something."

Nia bends and presses her lips over my heart. "I'm genuinely very glad you have them, but I wish I was there for you then. I wish I was there to tell you that *you* are what's important – to me, and to those who care about you."

"You've always been there, Nia," I say, then show her my tattoo. "I'd trace your name day and night while in the hospital. I kept thinking of what you must be up to, of how I could reach out to you, but I couldn't find a way to do it. I tried your old number, but it wasn't active. I tried looking you up on social media, but I couldn't find you anywhere. And, when I got discharged, I lost the little bravado I'd gathered to come here and see you myself."

She gives me a sad smile. "I wasn't exactly…nice to you during our last encounter all those years ago, so I don't blame you."

"It's not that," I assure her. "I guess I bailed on it because when I got out of the hospital, I realized that I didn't want you to know what I'd become in my haste of wanting to live up to others' expectations. I didn't want to, you know, disappoint you."

"You made a mistake, Cass, but you fixed it before it was too late."

"Sure, but I hated the guy I was during those few weeks," I concede.

"I'm sure that was just your mind's way of coping with the whole thing. Hate can be hurtful, but if it's temporary, it can help heal you." She rubs my arms. "I'm proud of you, and of all that you've achieved and lived through. I really am." She smiles openly. "Also, you wouldn't have disappointed me if you'd decided to come here and see me, just like you haven't disappointed me *now*. If anything, I'm honored that you chose to share something so sensitive with me, that you trusted me with it."

My throat tightens at her words; at the honesty on her face. "Thank you. It really means a lot to me. And it was pretty obvious for me to share this with you. I'm just sorry I didn't do it sooner."

"Hey, now; don't do that." She squeezes my hands. "Believe me when I say I get it. I really do."

"I know you do." I smile, then jerk my head towards the SUV that I parked just outside the field. "So, you ready for the impending dinner, then?" I ask.

Nia purses her lips in contemplation, then clicks her tongue before saying, "You know what? I think I am."

13.
nia

I wipe my palms over my jean-clad thighs and glance to my left. Cass is still busy browsing the menu booklet, whereas I – well, I'm close to choking on the suffocating air around us.

I have traded the dress I'd worn to the wedding for a pair of jeans and a grey sweater, and even though my outfit is supposed to be a reprise, I'm not exactly feeling comfortable sitting at a table for 3 at *Mama Peña's Diner*.

Mama Peña's Diner has been around for a while. It's a place every family in Adenbrooke frequents for wholesome meals and cozy vibes. With achievement awards framed to its stone walls, wooden furniture and leather couches that are simply the best, a vast kitchen area to the left that is viewable to the patrons, rock music blasting through the speakers, and large glass windows on the right that give a clear view of the town beyond, the diner is as perfect a place as it can get.

As if on cue, Mama Peña walks through the kitchen doors wearing her usual black trousers and a floral-print shirt, with her golden skin gleaming with sweat, and her long, black hair held behind her head in a ponytail. She briefly glances at Amanda, then raises her brows at me when our eyes meet.

I give her a vague shrug, to which she shakes her head, chuckles, and gets back to her customers.

I pull my hair into a low bun and frown at Cass, who is still looking at the damn menu. Him and I have spent dozens of evenings at the diner in the past, and even though Mama Peña has added a few new recipes to her list, they aren't *that* intriguing for him to be so lost in them that he can't even look up *once*.

Someone clears their throat – loud enough that I have no other choice but to look at them.

Amanda, dressed in a crisp black three-piece, with her short hair pin-straight, gives me a distasteful once-over, then turns her attention to Cass. "So, how was the wedding?" she asks him.

He finally places the menu on the table. "It was great." He clicks his tongue. "A little too colorful and flowery for my taste, but great nonetheless. It's actually the love between those guys that overpowered everything else, I'll say. They were *so* into each other that I'm sure they didn't give two shits about the people attending their wedding, *or* the decorations, for that matter." He looks at me. "It was beautiful witnessing them tie the knot, huh?"

It takes me a moment to find my voice.

"Yeah," I agree with a smile. "They are perfect for each other. It was wonderful seeing them make it official."

Cass grins. "Yeah, and–" He stops when his phone rings. "Sorry," he says around a chuckle, then glances at the name on the screen before quickly receiving the call. "Hey, Mom." The joy on his face was undeniable. "Yeah, I'm okay." He frowns. "Wait, what was that? Mom, I can't hear you." He's quiet as he tries to listen to what she's saying, then shakes his head. "No, you're breaking up; hold on a sec." He gets to his feet, gives me a quick kiss on the lips, then gives Amanda a 5-minutes gesture before making his way to the exit.

I watch as he pushes the diner's door open and steps into the street. Walking to the side, he says something into the phone, then laughs before talking in a way so animated, that it makes me smile.

"Stay *away* from him."

I whip my head at Amanda. "Excuse me?" I'm caught off guard by her sudden warning, but I try not to let it show on my face.

She crosses her arms across her chest. "You heard me perfectly fine the first time around, *Nia*. I don't think I'm inclined to repeat myself."

I lift a brow. "Oh, I *did*, but I would *love* it if you could tell me why you thought it was necessary for you to say that to me at all."

She sneers. "Don't try to act sassy with me. You and I both know this bubble of yours is going to burst the moment Cass leaves this God-awful town. If you think I'm going to let him stay here and ruin his career – one I've spent *years* helping him build – then you're too fucking naïve for your own loss. He's a star; he *commands* the social media with his presence. Do you even know how popular he is? Do you even know the number of fans he has?"

I have zero retorts for her questions. I don't know what to tell her, simply because I don't have the answer to anything she just asked me. Cass hasn't discussed his fame with me in detail, not really. He's only told me about the documentary, and that he trains Hollywood celebrities in fitness. I have no idea how famous he is, or the kind of power he has on social media. And due to the lack of this knowledge, I feel stupid sitting here looking at Amanda as she smirks victoriously at me, knowing she's gotten the upper hand on me.

"Yeah, that's what I thought," she states coolly. "You're just what I assumed you would be: a stupid *village girl* with dreams beyond her budget."

"What Cass and I have has nothing to do with fame and money," I say. "Him and I, we're–"

"Oh, do spare me your theatrics," she cuts me off. "Cass is an *idiot*. I've indulged his…itch for days now, let him play around as much as he wanted, but I've reached my limit. Now that our time here is coming to an end, I'm going to fix this mess so that there's nothing left for me to clean up after."

"It's not your place to manage his *personal* life, Amanda. You have no right to decide what he does and doesn't want. That's entirely his choice to make, not yours."

She laughs, and the sound pierces right through my ears. "Oh my God." She laughs some more. "Are you even listening to yourself right now?" She shakes her head. "I feel nothing but pity towards women like you, you know? Always hopeful and self-righteous. You think you deserve the best of everything just because you're poor and pray to God every night."

I grit my teeth as my anger rises, and glance at Cass, who is still busy on the phone.

"Is this why you agreed to have dinner with me – so that you could point out all the reasons why I don't deserve Cass?" I ask Amanda.

She places her elbows on the table and leans in. "You're a roadblock," she hisses. "You are a diversion he can't afford to have at this point in his career. Because all you will do is drag him down, and–"

"I would never do that to him," I tell her hotly. "I would never do anything to jeopardize his hard work. I respect his passion and appreciate everything he does."

"He deserves better, dammit!" she says loud enough that a few patrons turn to look at us. "Cass deserves so much better than you." She points a finger at me. "He deserves someone of his caliber, someone who can walk through society with him and he wouldn't feel embarrassed being seen with." She swallows and looks squarely at me. "He deserves someone like *me*."

I stare at her in complete disbelief. "Y…you?" I suck in a breath, and then, unable to hold it in, I chuckle. "Are you being serious right now?" I place a hand over my throat. "Cass sees you as a support system, Amanda, and *nothing else*." I chuckle again. "And you think *I'm* stupid."

"*How dare you?*" She slaps the table. "I know what I deserve, and what I deserve is *him*. I've given almost a decade of my life to him. I know him; I know what he should have. I know his tastes and preferences. I am *everything* he needs."

"And I know his *heart*," I say easily. "I'm pretty sure you don't know shit about that. You may know him on the surface, but I've known him for far longer than you have, and I'm positive that he'd want nothing to do with you if he knew the kind of person you really are."

"Are you threatening me, you worthless *bitch*?" She leans closer. "Are you sure you wanna do that? Because I can end you in a minute; I can destroy you and your family with a blink of an eye."

I'm taken aback by the pure malice on her face, and my head feels heavy at the seriousness in her voice.

She means it. She really fucking means it.

"I'm glad you've understood that I'm not bullshitting you, Nia. I *will* ruin you and your loved ones if you don't back off." She sits back in her chair and assesses me with narrowed eyes.

"Who is threatening who, now?" I sneer.

"You think you're smart, don't you? Let's see how well that tongue of yours will help you once I'm done teaching your family a lesson for your arrogance."

I fist my hands when they start shaking. "You *wouldn't*."

"I will if you continue to act like a rebel and disagree to get out of Cass's life."

"You have *no* right to–"

"Do you wanna know what would happen if *Café Connell* were to suddenly go out of business?" she asks calmly. "Isn't that…quaint little thing the only source of income for your family, Nia?"

Bile rises in the back of my throat.

Amanda latches onto my inability to speak, and smirks. "Have you imagined what would happen if customers stopped showing up to your café, and your financial numbers plummeted as a result of that? What would that do to your business-oriented brother and retired parents? Have you thought about any of it?"

"How do you…" I clear my throat. "How do you know all this?"

She snickers. "You think I haven't been doing my research? When Cass introduced you to me yesterday, I knew you were the Nia he's had a tattoo of on his wrist for all these years. I just *had* to know all about you, and so, I did. Didn't take long, to be honest, given there's hardly anything to you and your…*life*. Your ex-husband was more than willing to spill the details to me after a few rounds of beer. Good-looking guy, by the way. A pity you let him go. You two must've looked quite adorable during your time together, I'm sure."

I glare at her. "Well, why don't you have *him*, then? You two would fit right in – you know, with being venomous snakes and all."

"Careful, girl." She pulls her phone out of her fancy clutch. "One call, and you'll be done for. I don't make idle threats, so you better watch your mouth."

I glance at her phone, then at Cass. He scratches the back of his head and chuckles at something his mom must've said to him. The happiness on his face, the spark in his eyes – they make me want to choke on my damn fate. *He* makes me want to fall to my knees and beg the Lord to help me find a way.

A way for me to not be in the situation I currently am.

A way for me to come up with something – *anything* – to keep my normalcy, and *him*, by my side. A way for me to rise above Amanda's crude promises.

But…as I keep looking at the man who is the very foundation of my newfound, rocky little empire with hot, helpless tears running down my eyes, I can't, for the life of me, think of anything that will help us get what we really want.

"You don't come for those I care about, and I'll do as you asked," I tell Amanda, feeling an ache building in my chest.

"You have my word," she answers with a slight tilt of her head.

I avert my gaze from her as I push back my chair and get to my feet. Holding onto the edge of the table when a wave of dizziness hits me, I manage not to rock on my feet, and then, once I'm sure I won't fall, I sidestep a server and walk away from Amanda.

I've only just stepped out of the diner when Cass turns, still on the phone. He looks at me, and the smile vanishes almost immediately from his face. He makes as if to come to me, but I move back, turn around, and run away from him.

"Nia!" he calls out, panic clear in his voice. "Nia, wait!"

I don't. I *can't*. I keep running, and running, and run–

"Ouch!" I exclaim when I bump into something.

"The *hell*, Nia?" Bran says.

I look up at him, and try to simmer down my rage when a sudden urge to punch a hole in his chest takes over me. This dickwad is the reason Amanda humiliated me so easily, tried to break me with words and threats I had no counter for.

But…

"Do you have your motorcycle with you?" I ask him. He's the last person I want to ask for help, especially when all I want to do is cause him physical pain, but right now, I have no other choice but to turn a donkey into a horse.

"What?" He furrows his brows in confusion.

"Your motorcycle, you dumbass – do you have it with you?"

He scowls. "Don't talk to me like that."

I huff. "Get over yourself, will you? I'm not in the mood for your superiority complex bullshit."

He scans my face – my tearstained, crestfallen face – and his expression softens slightly, which does surprise me a little, if not much.

"Yeah, I do," he tells me.

"Drop me at my house," I say to him. "And if you ask any stupid questions along the way, I swear to God I'll choke you with your own dick. Trust me, that's all my brain is thinking of right now, so don't even try to test me."

He looks at me for a long moment, then puts his tongue to his cheek before nodding at me. "Fine, then; no questions." He jerks his head to the side. "Come on, let's get you home."

14.
cass

Tires skid against the slushy ground as I stop the SUV outside the gate, then open the driver's side door before running over to her house. The lights in the living room are on, which means that she's home. I cross the fence, and am about to climb the porch stairs when the front door opens, and out marches an angry Noah.

"The fuck you want, Madden?" he all but spits the question at me. Even though we're the same height, the guy has at least 3 times more muscle on me. "You come here to get your teeth punched in or somethin'?"

I sigh and raise my hands in front of me. "Look, I just wanna talk to her, okay? She didn't even stop to tell me what happened, Noah. I'm fucking worried." The entire drive from the diner to Nia's place was a dizzying blur. Fear and confusion rode each of my shoulders, and the possibility that I'd screwed everything up *again* – yeah, that shit was, and *is*, right on top of my list of concerns.

Noah glares at me. "Your manager happened, Cass."

I open and shut my mouth. "What?"

He pushes back his hair. "Do you seriously want me to believe that you don't know how Arianna, or whatever the fuck your manager's name is, threatened my baby sister? That she said she'd ruin my family if Nia didn't stay away from you? Do you honestly not know the way that woman treated Nia when she stood up for herself? Come on, Madden, you can't be that dense."

I stand there looking at him like an immobile piece of shit.

"Amanda did *what*?" It's pathetic how helpless I sound. I guess, in a way, it *is* my fault that my manager is so stupidly cruel. But this…

"That Amanda lady's got a thing for you, dude," Noah tells me with disdain. "She told Nia as much. Said she deserved to be by your side instead of my sister." He shakes his head. "This is so messed up. I knew I should have interfered when you started seeing Nia again. I knew I should have separated you two the moment you got your hands on her a second time. But I didn't have the balls, especially after seeing her so happy about the fact that you were back." He wipes a hand over his face and looks at me. "But what's done is done, and *this*…" He points at me, and then at the house. "It's over. Whatever you had with her – it's finished now. I'm not going to let this get any more painful for her than it already is. She deserves better than what happened tonight, and you and I both know that."

My throat is so tight that I'm scared I might choke, but I swallow and make myself speak. "Please let me see her, man," I all but beg. "Just for 5 minutes – that's all I'm asking for."

"I can't," Noah says with a frown. "And I'll ask you not to put me in a position where I really have to live up to my warning of punching you. Because I *will* do it if you force my hand and not leave, Cass. She's my family, and I'll do everything I can to keep her from another heartbreak. She's been through a lot over the years. Just…just please don't add to her stress. She doesn't need that, especially not right now."

My jaw tingles as I sniff. "She means *everything* to me, Noah," I whisper. "You fucking *know* that."

"Do I?" His expression hardens again, and when I don't respond to him, because I really don't know how else to make him understand that I'm not lying to him, he scoffs and starts walking backwards. "Go back to your manager and flashy lifestyle, Madden. It's the only language you know, and the only thing you'll ever understand. Adenbrooke and its simplicity are no longer your forte. This town – it's no longer your home." And with that, he swivels on his feet and marches into the house before shutting the door behind him.

15.
cass

I bang a fist against Amanda's door for the third consecutive time, and finally hear unhurried footsteps on the other side. As I wait for her to open up, I shift from one foot to the other in hopes of taming my haywire nerves. I know she's deliberately delaying facing me, but I'll wait. Because she can't stay locked in her room forever, whereas I – I can stand here for as long as it'll take for her to come to terms with the fact that she has no other choice but to look me in the eyes and tell me how royally she has fucked things up for me.

The door finally swings open. "Cass? Is everything okay?" she asks, and has the absolute *audacity* of looking oblivious.

"Apart from your unwarranted performance at the diner, you mean?" I sneer at her.

She places the book she's holding on the nightstand, then sets her glasses atop it. "What are you talking about?" Her voice is hard now. Irritated, even.

I sneer at her. "Are we *really* doing this right now, Amanda?" I shake my head a little. "We aren't in a damn soap opera, so can you please stop with the whole '*I don't know what you're talking about*' bullshit with me. Because I know that you're aware of what you've done."

She stares at me with an intensity which, a few years ago would have made me uncomfortable, but now? Yeah, it's doing nothing to me.

"What I did, I did it in order to protect your career," she states tersely.

"Oh, did you now?" I counter. "Could have fooled me."

Her nostrils flare as the expression on her face contorts. "That girl is *not* the right match for you and the status you hold."

"And *you* are, Amanda?" I take a step towards her. "Nia is the wrong choice, but *you're* the perfect one? Is that what it is?"

She clenches her jaw as she looks at me. "I've given *years* of my life to you," she says a bit hoarsely. "*Years*, Cass. I built you; I built your brand. I made you who you are, and I won't let some inane *village girl* ruin everything I've worked so hard on. There's no chance I would have let her take the fruits of my labor."

I'm stunned by her words, by the crazy gleam in her eyes.

"Are you even listening to yourself right now?" I tell her. "You sound delusional, Amanda. While I appreciate everything you've done for me, I'm not a goddamn prize horse you can bait into obeying you by doing good on me. Everything you helped me achieve, you did it because I hired you to do so. And up until an hour ago, I had nothing but respect for you, and for your unrelenting hustle. But this…" I gesture vaguely in her direction. "Did you really think your behavior towards Nia would make me want you?" And here I am – a dumb fuck – thinking that she'd *saved* me 3 years ago. How I thought she was the one who pulled me out of that phase because she genuinely cared. If only I'd known how wrong her intentions had been all along, things would have been different now.

How the fuck had I been so stupid?

"I'm delusional because I'm an ambitious woman who knows what she wants and has the means to achieve it?" she hisses, making me look at her.

"*Achieve* it?" I back away from her, because what the fuck? "Am I a thing to be obtained? Because last I checked, I'm a man who has the liberty of making his own choices. I don't need anyone deciding what is best for me and my life. I don't want anyone ruling things out for me so that I can follow a parallel line and lead a life that isn't mine to control."

"But I know what you deserve," she says with insistence, and gets close to me. "You deserve someone who thinks the way you do; someone who reciprocates your goals and dreams. Cass, you need someone who'll walk beside you knowing full well what is expected of you. You need someone who won't hold you back or affect your flow of work." She swallows. "You need someone who *belongs to your world*." She reaches out a hand to touch my forearm, but I step away.

"Don't," I warn.

Anger flashes across her face. "What do you even *see* in her?" She runs her fingers through her hair. "She's a *café owner* with no status in the society, no importance. She's nothing but another face in the crowd, whereas I," she points at herself, "I'm powerful, influential. I know what you want. I'll *always* know what you want." She looks crazed, almost like she's overcome by her own words, and believes them to be completely true.

"I never imagined I'd ever say this to you, but you've proved everything I thought I knew about you to be wrong, so I have no other choice but to tell you that you're *pathetic*, Amanda. I've treated you with nothing but admiration since the day we met, but today, you put an end to that by acting the way you did, and by saying the things you said." I let go of a short breath. "Nia…she's nothing like you. She doesn't bribe someone to be in a relationship with her because she's got a few numbers on her phone that belong to some hotshot people higher up in the social world. She doesn't need to be *powerful* or *influential* to be herself. She doesn't need threats and insults to show her dominance. She shines just by being herself. She outnumbers everyone just by being who she is. She is important to *me*; she's everything I *want* and *deserve*."

"You're acting like a child," Amanda spits out. "You're being immature and foolish. What you feel for Nia is nothing but a crush. But what you and I have – that's something entirely different."

A crude laugh leaves me, and it's so sudden that it makes her jerk a little. "*What you and I have?*" I laugh again. "I'm sorry, but what *do* we have, Amanda? Have I ever given you any kind of a sign? Have my words towards you ever been suggestive? I most definitely don't think so. And that's because I've never even *considered* the possibility of us. I've always seen you as a mentor – someone I wouldn't…" I shake my head. "You know what?

Forget it. I don't think anything I'm saying right now is getting through to you anyway."

"You're lying." She gives me a once over before waving a hand at me. "I know you feel it. I've seen it in your eyes whenever we're together. I've seen the looks you–"

"You're simply proving my point, Amanda. Nothing I just told you got through to you." This version of her is something I never, for the life of me, expected to see.

"You're denying what we have because I took care of that bitch?" she asks. "She had it coming; she was dreaming too big and had to be shown the fu–"

"Just *stop*," I sneer, then grit my teeth. "You did something you had no right to. Your interference in my lif–"

"I am your *manager*, Cass," she says in a raised voice. "I am your goddamn manag–"

"*Were*," I cut her off.

She pales, staring at me with hollow eyes. "Excuse me?"

"You *were* my manager, Amanda," I clarify. "You're fired; I am no longer in need of your services."

"You can't possibly mean that."

"But I *do*." I bend a little and get in her face. "I need you out of this B&B by tomorrow morning. My lawyers will settle the last of your salary and book you a flight back to NYC in an hour, tops. The tour buses are occupied as I have a bit more filming to do, so you'll be traveling through air this time." I straighten. "Oh, and one more thing," I say with a slight smirk. "You'll be completely cut off from my work management and schedules, and papers will be drafted for the same so as to avoid any future confusion or conflict."

She seethes. "You will be *nothing* without me. You'll be ruined and unguided – left for the dogs to piss on. You will be wiped away from the history of social influencers without my help and connections."

I click my tongue. "If I were you, I'd worry about *my* future more than anyone else's, because Amanda…" I assess her from head to toe. "I am most definitely *not* going to stay quiet about what you did tonight. I will not let you fuck up another person's life with your toxicity and madness. You need help, and as much as I wanna say that I'll get it for you, I don't think I want to get involved in anything that has to do with you – not anymore." Before she can say anything, I turn on my heels and walk away from her.

I march into my room and pull my phone out of my pocket, and don't even think twice before pressing call on Nia's number. My heart is in my throat as I wait for the call to connect, but when it goes straight to voicemail, I press the back of my head against the door and close my eyes.

"Fuck," I whisper into the darkness of my room, then sit my ass on the floor, because really, what else am I even supposed to do right now?

16.
nia

"**G**ood morning, bitch!" Emma screeches through the other end of the line.

I frown, eyes still closed, and shift in my queen-sized bed. "Ugh. Why are you so chirpy this early in the morning?"

"Early?!" She sounds almost offended, which makes me smile a little. "It's 10-fucking-a.m., Nia. TEN! Did you sleep upside down last night?"

"No, you weirdo, I just slept real late." I huff and scratch the back of my thigh through my raised oversized t-shirt. "Noah let me take a few more days to myself before I can go back to the café, so I'm taking advantage of that. He said he didn't want me looking like a heartbroken zombie while serving our gossip-hungry customers, so he wants me to figure my shit out before I can step into the shop again. Didn't I tell you all of this on the phone yesterday, though?"

She clicks her tongue. "You did, but I forgot. Also, your brother is an asshole for keeping you away from work. I can't imagine a better breakup remedy than snorting freshly pressed coffee beans up your nose. It's quite literally the ultimate medicine."

My chest tightens at her words, but I brush off the feeling before it can take over, because I can't always be strong enough to deal with the pain that comes along with it. Sometimes I just need to be able to breathe without having to brace myself for an attack, or worse, a mental wound.

Most scars vanish over time, stop hurting as they age into our skin. Maybe mine would, too, despite them not being physical ones.

I rub my eyes. "My head hurts; let me go back to sleep."

"Why the hell did you even receive my call if you didn't wanna talk?"

"Because you kept calling insistently and I had no other choice but to answer you?"

Silence, and then… "I did?" she asks innocently, which makes me chuckle.

"You're incorrigible," I say.

She laughs, and then sneezes. "Sorry."

"Bless you." I yawn and straighten in bed, which results in my t-shirt to rise above my thighs. My eyes immediately go to the open window above the study table on the right, and sure enough, I find my neighbor's son, Bob, ogling me with a hand inside his pants.

Fucking perv.

Trying to avoid any and every encounter with Cass has led me to confining myself in my house. It has also led to Bob getting a front-row view of me sleeping in every day, and despite being an annoying one, it isn't the most important issue in my life.

Noah has given me my unquestioned space after the diner fiasco, which I honestly really appreciate. It wasn't easy reliving each and every one of Amanda's words and trying to put ample meaning to them, but I've spent hours upon hours on them anyway. At one point, I even considered the possibility of Cass being the one behind this. That maybe he was done with me, and because he couldn't ditch me *again*, he'd asked his manager to do the job for him. And, Amanda being Amanda, she'd kicked things up a notch by not only delivering his message, but to also shaming me in the process.

It makes no sense, obviously, and I don't know why I'm scared of confronting Cass about this. Instead of talking to him, I've been ignoring his calls and messages. I know that whatever Amanda said to me at *Mama Peña's Diner* was all her. I just know it. Her words, her expressions, and her general disdain towards me – that's all *her*, not Cass. And yet, I just can't bring myself to speak to him, even though I want nothing more than to touch him, hold him, and kiss him again.

My stubbornness is stupid and uncalled for, but I do need time to myself so that I can…process everything, in a way.

Cass has fired Amanda. He'd texted me as much a little over a week ago. I'm not sure if it was right for me to feel satisfied after having read that message, but I don't care. I don't know her well, but I know she isn't someone Cass needs, professionally or otherwise.

"That creep is staring at me again," I tell Emma in order to get rid of the thoughts in my head, and curse when Bob starts jerking himself harder when our eyes meet. That bald and bearded caveman-looking asshole has no fucking shame.

"Ewww." Emma gags through the line. "Please tell me you're going to at least show him the finger, if not report him to the authorities."

"He's harmless, Em."

"For *now*."

I sigh. "His dad's a decent guy; a family friend. And that puts me under an obligation of sorts."

"An obligation of letting his middle-aged son jerk off to you?" Emma questions incredulously.

I rise, press my phone between my ear and shoulder, and tie my hair into an overhead bun before walking towards the window. "I don't know what else you want me to say to you."

"I want you to tell me why you don't show him the finger," she pushes.

"I do!" I say. "I fucking do, Em, but I think that just turns him on even more."

"Ohmygod," she mutters. "That's…questionably gross."

I chuckle. "Right?" I slide the window shut with a *bang*. Glancing once at a still-jerking-off Bob, I flash him the middle finger and quickly pull the curtains close.

"You flipped him off, didn't you?" Emma asks.

I laugh as I face the dressing-table mirror. "Emma Rose Smith, are you accusing me of indecent behavior?"

"I'm *confirming*. There's a difference."

I click my tongue and stare at my reflection. My eyes look…dull against the warm ambience of my room. My cheeks are a bit hollow, my jaw sharper. Pair that with super dry lips and dark circles, and I'm ready to break into Hollywood as the female version of Michael Myers.

I sigh and shake my head. "Do you think I should tell Noah?" I question.

"About Bob?"

"Yeah," I say. "This has been going on for days now. Usually I'm up early and already at work, so we don't see each other. But now that I'm home..."

"He's been creaming his pants to your luscious body?"

I scowl. "Please never use those words in the same sentence again. Better yet, don't use them at all."

"But you love me," she quips.

I roll my eyes. "I do, *unfortunately*."

She chuckles. "Okay, so, to answer your question: if you *really* wanna see Bob lifeless and in a coffin wearing a too-tight three-piece, then go right ahead and tell your brother everything. I mean, have you seen Noah's biceps? I bet his fist is larger than Bob's head."

I can't help but laugh. "You're *married*, Em, in case you forgot. Keeping mental measurements of my brother's body is hardly appropriate for you."

"Meh, it's fine. Martin knows he married a weirdo."

I grin. "You–"

"Honey!" comes Mom's voice from the living room.

"Ah, shoot. Hey, Em, my mom's here. I promised I'd help her and Dad in cleaning their house today." I walk over to my closet and pull out a pair of jeans and a plain yellow t-shirt. "I gotta go, babe."

"Of course! I have to go check on Megan anyway. Have to make sure she hasn't moved from having a normal phone call with her boyfriend to having phone sex with him."

I stop in my tracks. "I'm sorry, what?"

Emma sighs. "Megan has a boyfriend, Nia. Keep up."

"*She's 5 years old*," I say in complete disbelief, making sure to emphasize each word.

"Well, her generation moves fast. You and I waited too long, apparently."

"I…" I shake my head.

"Nia, honey? You here?" Mom calls out.

"Yeah, Mom; gimme 10. I need to dress up."

"Sure thing!" I hear her humming and moving around in the living room, which puts a smile on my face.

"Go help your parents while I go sneak up on my spawn," Emma tells me.

I chuckle. "Does Martin know?"

"Have you seen his face flashing on your TV screen for homicide yet?"

I cough behind a fist. "No?"

"Yeah, so he doesn't know."

"You're–"

"Crazy, I know; you've said that before."

I grin. "Alright, gotta go. Thank you for cheering me up. It means a lot; love you."

"Don't mention it. I've got you, babe. Take as much time as you need to feel better, and once you're sure you're ready, *talk to him*." She clears her throat. "Before it's too late."

Before he goes back to New York, is what she means.

I enter the bathroom. "I will, I promise."

I have to, right? I gave him a second chance, and he did everything to live up to it; respected the risk I took on him. Until Amanda happened. It would be stupid if I let him go again without a proper conversation. He most definitely doesn't deserve that, and neither do I.

"Good," Emma states. "So, I'll see you at Gerald and Jasper's party tonight?"

I smile and grab my toothbrush. "Yeah, I'll be there."

17.
nia

"I have never seen a girl as pretty as you," Bob says, and makes as if to lean in, but stumbles sideways when Emma pushes him.

"Oopsies; my bad," she sings as she gives Bob a clinical smile.

He huffs and rights himself, then looks at me again. "So, I was thinking maybe you'd like to–"

"Nope," I cut him off, keeping my gaze, and my complete attention, on something that is happening only a few feet from me.

"But–"

"Not gonna happen, Bob, so beat it," I state without facing him, and get more comfortable in the chair I'm sitting in.

Ger and Jas's party is in the back garden of their beautiful house. The setup isn't as grand and decorative out here as it had been on their wedding day; it's more cozy, comfortable, and serene – something I really appreciate.

A gentle breeze whips by me, bringing with it the smell of crisp snow, and the beautiful catnips Gerald grows in his back garden.

As I glance around the area, I find Ger grilling steak with some of the guests, whereas Jas – whose company I have yet to be graced with today – is in the kitchen with his book club friends.

The kids present at the party are either pre-teens running around chasing each other, or horny teenagers trying to come across as subtle as they check each other out. The adults, however, are busy discussing their businesses with suffocating interest.

And I? Well, I'm manning the refreshments table to make sure the sassy, adrenaline-induced kids don't grab alcohol from underneath it. And also to make sure they get at least 1 glass of Jas's special lemonade.

Now *that's* the dream job, isn't it?

The day has set, and I'm both tired of smiling at townies, and frustrated by the lack of alcohol in my body. I have to stay sober so that I can tend to the minors without looking like I took a dip in a pool of Jack Daniels.

Bob mutters something under his breath, but doesn't move away from the table.

2 schoolgirl-like giggles make me flinch. I know who they belong to. I've been looking at its owners for the last few minutes, after all.

Clary and Chloe Williams. The mayor's twin daughters.

With legs for days, creamy skin, long, raven-black hair, bright green eyes, and the similar-looking too-short black dresses the two are wearing, they look ready to walk a runway, not attend a house party.

Only 25 years old, Clary and Chloe are established businesswomen who run a successful boutique in Adenbrooke. They're considered as "style icons" around town, according to Bob. And those very "style icons" are currently glued to Cass's side, all but slithering over him like leeches.

It's not like I'm keeping tabs on him or anything, but I can't deny the fact that I got all jittery and restless when Gerald told me he'd invited the '*hot fellow*' I'd attended his wedding with, to the party tonight.

I'd been shocked to see Cass walking in through the open patio doors an hour ago, but I'd tried not to act too affected by his presence. It was hard not to show, but I'd tried.

When our eyes had met, he'd been the first to look away, and when Ger had asked him to join him for a drink, I'd gone back to serving lemonade to the kids, and beer to the adults.

"Glaring murderously in their direction won't make them vanish, you know," Emma says to me.

I blink and face her. "What?"

She rolls her eyes. "Don't act dumb, Nia; you know what I'm talking about."

I shift in my seat, then look at Cass and the twin leeches again.

Wearing a white Henley, a black winter coat, dark grey jeans, and black boots, he looks too good for the very air around us. His hair is damp and tied loosely at the back of his head, which only added to his seamless appearance.

I clear my throat and drag my eyes away from him. "What else can I do, Em? I can't help myself when it comes to him." I bring my hair over a shoulder. "My eyes keep going back to him even when I try not to let them."

She exhales a puff of air. "I get it, babe; I do. But you promised you'd enjoy yourself today, so maybe focus on that a little bit. And I know he hasn't approached you yet, but that's okay. You can be the one to do it later, can't you? Wait for a while and see how things go, though. Maybe he's looking for a spare moment to steal you away, or maybe he's just a dick. Either way, it's his loss, really. There's plenty of other dicks in the sea. Take your pick and go to town with it. Pun *totally* intended on the town thing."

"I agree," Bob says enthusiastically.

I sigh. "Of course you do."

He shrugs, and I point a finger at Emma. "First of all, it's plenty of *fish* in the sea, not *dicks*. But thanks to you, I now can't get the image of floating dicks out of my head." When her and Bob laugh, I flip them off. "And second of all, I'm totally enjoying myself right now, what with serving drinks to this thirsty crowd and all." I glance at said crowd, then purse my lips. "But in all honesty, I don't know what the fuck I'm doing." I grab a glass of lemonade and down it in one go. "I just fucking don't." I throw the empty glass into the bin and glare at Clary and Chloe, who have their arms wrapped around Cass's.

"You need alcohol, Nia, not lemonade," Emma muses as she smirks at me.

"Fuck you," I grumble.

She chuckles, and so does Bob.

Great. At least I'm capable of providing free entertainment to people.

Emma opens her mouth to say something, when suddenly, *Desire*, by Sam Smith and Calvin Harris, starts playing on the speakers set up on the porch.

I look around, and find Gerald fiddling with the laptop that's connected to the speakers.

Emma arches a brow at me. "That old nugget sure does know his shit." She then turns to her husband, who is busy chatting up a work friend. "Hon, you wanna dance?"

He grins at her. "You know I do."

The two reach the center of the garden and start jumping and singing along with the song. To no one's surprise, almost everyone joins them. Well, all except for the senior members in attendance.

The kids jump and squeal; the adults dance as awkwardly as they'd be expected to. Clary and Chloe drag Cass into the crowd, and I watch, while fuming immaturely, as they twirl and circle around him like starving harpies. He places his hands on one of the twin's waist and gives her a small smile, then chuckles when the other leaps on his back, which makes the kids go wild.

I clear my throat and look at Bob, who is smiling fondly at the scene before us.

"Hey, Bob."

He faces me, still all smiles. "Yeah?"

"You wanna dance?" I ask.

His eyes widen. He opens and closes his mouth multiple times, then scratches his head. "You…you wanna *dance*…with *me*?"

"Mm-hm."

He adjusts the collar of his blue shirt, then fixes the poor belt that is barely clinging to his beer-belly. "Why yes, I would love to!"

I chuckle and get to my feet. "Well, let's go fucking dance, then, shall we?"

18.
cass

Fucking Bob. Nia is dancing with *Bob*.

I saw them joining everyone on the "dance floor" a while ago. I saw the bastard acting all goofy around her; saw her laugh at his silly moves. And I sure as hell noticed how she purposefully avoided looking at me, even though we were standing *right next to each other*.

Fucking *Bob*.

He runs his dad's garage, is unmarried, has no kids, and has had his sights set on Nia since her and I were fifteen. You'd think the age difference would have affected the way he looked at her back then, but nope. He was a perv, through and through, and it's pretty clear things haven't changed for him, even now.

When Nia and I's eyes had met for the first time in days a few minutes ago, she'd been standing behind the serving table. My stupid heart had done a fucking tumble after seeing her, because God, she's absolutely *breathtaking*. The color of her sweater is the exact same as the blush on her cheeks. Pair that with faded jeans and brown boots, and she's the most beautiful person in the crowd. And her long hair, open and flowing with the wind like it always is, makes me wanna run my fingers through it.

I'd been the first to look away. She'd seemed shocked to see me, which'd led me to believe that maybe Gerald hadn't told her that I'd be attending the party.

"So, Chase," says Clary, pulling me out of my thoughts. Or is it Chloe? I have no damn idea. "You'll come check out our racks tomorrow, won't you? I promise you that our collection is the best in Adenbrooke."

I flinch a little and face the twins. They don't just say my name incorrectly – *every damn time*, despite me having corrected them more than once – but they also emphasize the word 'rack' whenever they use it in a sentence. I know that there's a very high bar of ignorance, combined with stupidity out there in the world, but just how fucking dumb does one have to be to not remember a simple *name*, or even behave like they aren't coming on to someone too hard?

I *really* want to know.

"Chase?" the other twin says loudly when she thinks I haven't heard her sister over the sound of the music.

I blink and flash her a smile. "Yeah?" This is exactly what I've been doing for almost an hour: smiling, being polite, and trying not to bang my head against a wall.

Clary/Chloe grins and steps closer to me. "You'll come check out our clothing *racks*, right? I think some of our designs will look *perfect* on you."

Jesus, if you're up there, please tie me to a fucking anchor and drown me into an endless ocean.

"Chase?"

I'm close to losing my shit. *Completely*.

"I'll have to take this up with my designer, ladies," I reply as politely as I can. "If he agrees to it, then I'll have him come check out your collection for potential outfits."

Clary and Chloe look blankly at me. "But can't you just come and do that yourself?"

"I hardly shop fashion these days, what with my busy schedule. It's difficult to balance everything out, hence I have a designer."

"But–"

I put on my professional face. "Javier is excellent at what he does, I promise. He's the perfect person to come look at your stuff."

They open their mouths to say something, but I turn around, only to find *Bob* with his hands pressed to the sides of Nia's waist.

Fucking dipshit.

He bends to say something in her ear, which makes her laugh.

I clench and unclench my fists, feeling annoyingly frustrated.

She should be dancing with *me*, but instead, she won't even glance my way.

Fucking fantastic.

Something small hits the side of my head. I hiss a curse and look down, only to find some plastic toy fallen at my feet. I then look in the direction from which it had come, and see Gerald, seated in a chair a few feet from me, with a beer bottle in one hand and a freakish-looking toy in the other, ready to hit me with it again.

"*What the fuck, Gerald?*" I mouth.

He huffs and drops the toy, then fishes his phone out of his pocket. Tapping on the screen for a while, and then places the phone to his ear, and I feel mine begin to vibrate in my jeans a couple of seconds later.

"I repeat: what the fuck, Gerald?" I say by way of greeting.

He glares at me. "What're you doing, you dickwad?"

"What?" He has to stop drinking, or else he'll seriously injure someone.

"You're letting Bob steal your girl," he grumbles.

My brows furrow in confusion. "Wait, how do you kno–"

"You aren't exactly being subtle about it, Cass," he provides. "And neither is she."

I sigh and run a hand over my jaw. "Everything is fucked, Ger. Hell, I don't even know if she's my girl anymore. Or if she even *wants* to be mine anymore."

The old rug scowls at me. "And whose fault is that?"

I roll my eyes. "Why did you hit me? Couldn't you have simply called me, like you did *after* almost giving me a concussion?"

He smirks. "Where would the fun in that be?"

I snort. "So, you stole some poor kid's toys for what, fun? Your idea of fun is making people lose consciousness?"

He flips me off, which makes me chuckle. "I didn't steal them. I *borrowed* them."

"Uh-huh, whatever you say."

He glares at me. *Again*. "Go get her, Cass, before Bob puts a fucking ring on it or somethin'."

I quickly glance at Nia and Bob, who are still laughing and dancing, then look at Gerald again. "Well, he might as well. She seems really happy right now."

Gerald makes to throw his beer bottle at me, and on instinct, I take a step back. "Stop being so goddamn insufferable, boy. Get your ass in gear and *do* something. Get that bald fucking caveman away from Nia."

"Jesus, how much have you had to drink, Ger? You sound like my dead grandma, man. May the lord rest her soul."

He huffs again. "*Go. Do. Something.*"

"Fine." I raise a hand when he again threatens to attack me with the beer bottle. "I'm going; I'm going. Fucking contain yourself, dude." I disconnect the call and slide my phone into my back pocket.

Gerald grins and gives me a thumbs up, which makes me smile and shake my head at him.

I look around, but can't find the Williams twins, which is a relief.

Good riddance.

With a deep inhale and a quick exhale, I step forward and place a hand on Bob's shoulder.

Here goes.

19.
cass

"Hey, Bob. What's up, buddy?"

Nia sucks in a breath when she sees me, but then quickly looks away.

Bob, with sweat dripping down his head, faces me. "Hey, Cass." He smiles. "All's good here. How have you been? Man, the last time I saw you, you were a skinny 16-year-old trying to finish assignments and pass class."

Get your hands off of Nia, I want to say, but don't. What I instead do is chuckle, if only to indulge him. "*Yup*, that was me," I say lightly. "But things have changed now, haven't they?" I slide my hands into the pockets of my jeans and give him a slight shrug. "Anyway. How's your stomach these days? I was just talking to your dad a few minutes ago, and he said you've been having digestion issues lately." Being cornered by Davis just to be told about his son's…problems wasn't exactly on the list of things I wanted to hear in my lifetime, but eh, how could I stop a father from vividly describing his son's bowel issues to me?

Bob finally lets go of Nia and turns to me. "Yeah, Dad's pretty worried. I have problems after I eat food, be it any meal. It doesn't really go down well, you know? Acidity, nausea, etc. Thanks for asking, man."

"Yeah, no worries."

Bob and I smile at each other for a painfully long moment, and I feel Nia shifting on her feet, clearly uncomfortable with the situation she's found herself stuck in.

Some new pop song blasts through the speakers, which makes the kids jump and scream in excitement.

"So, uh…" I clear my throat. "Can I borrow Nia for a while?" I ask Bob. "There's something I need to talk to her about."

Bob looks between her and I, then lifts a shoulder. "Sure, of course." He steps back. "Uh, hey, I would really appreciate if you could help me pick some easy exercises that I can do in order to fix my…"

"Metabolism issue?" I provide.

Bob looks sheepish as he nods. "Yeah, that. I'll pay a fee for it."

I wave a hand at him. "Not necessary. I'll email you my self-designed beginner's workout routine *and* an easy diet regime tomorrow. Follow them for three months with no skips, and then email me about your progress so that I can upgrade both plans accordingly."

He seems genuinely grateful. "Thanks, man."

I shake my head. "Don't mention it."

What? I'm not a bad guy, okay? The things Bob is facing are detrimental to his health, and I really want to help him in any way I can.

Him and I exchange email addresses, before he turns around and faces Nia again. "Holler if you need me," he tells her quietly, but I hear it anyway.

Seriously? *Holler if you need me?* That's what he says right after I agree to help him with his…unhealthy stomach?

Fan-fucking-tastic.

I watch as Bob walks over to the drink table, sits in the chair that's behind it, and gets busy on his phone.

A true savior, indeed.

"*How's your stomach?* Really? That's the best you've got?" Nia says, then crosses her arms over her chest.

I look down at her. Tiny flakes of snow have settled on her hair and lashes, and the blush on her cheeks has now deepened to a lovely shade of red.

"What, you didn't think I was being on-brand and shit?" I ask.

She tilts her head a little, and in that exact instant, moonlight hits her side profile, making her appear even more beautiful than she already is.

She scoffs. "So, what did you wanna talk about, then?"

I take a step towards her, and smirk when she doesn't step back. Her chest rises and falls faster than normal, and her lips part as she keeps looking up at me with her all-seeing eyes.

"You know exactly what I wanna talk about," I tell her, then hold onto her waist before pulling her to me. "But the real question is: are *you* ready to talk about it?" The smell of her honey-sweet perfume hits me with full force, giving me a sense of both nostalgia and longing.

Time is not on my side when it comes to her and I. My team wrapped up filming the other day, and I can only pretend to want to stay in Adenbrooke for so long before my lawyers decide to come here and drag my ass back to New York. They're currently hard at work finding me a new, mentally stable manager. It's tough, obviously, but not impossible.

I *have* to settle things here; I have to know where Nia and I stand.

I *need* to know what she wants, and what is to become of us.

She doesn't flinch or move away from my touch, and instead, gently presses her palms to my chest. "Cass…" She blinks, then releases a soft puff of air as she exhales.

I bend and bring my face close to hers. She feels so fucking amazing, like silk-smooth warmth and blissful familiarity, and I'm the lucky bastard who gets to witness it all, standing right here under the glimmering sky with her.

"God, you're gorgeous," I say to her. "What the *hell* was I thinking when I decided to stay away from you in order to give you your goddamn space? Fuck, woman."

She's trying not to smile, I can tell. "You've *always* laid it on too thick, haven't you?"

I chuckle. "I wouldn't be me if I didn't."

Her lips twitch. "And what a shame that'd be."

"It's the truth – what I just said. But I'll tone it down for you if you want."

Nia's eyes search my face, just as mine search hers. "Have I ever wanted that from you?" she questions.

I shake my head. "Not really, no."

Another song starts playing at an awfully loud volume, which makes Nia grimace.

"Can we…" She scowls at the screaming kids, who instantly shut up when they see her expression. With a sigh, she then looks at me. "Can we go somewhere quiet where we can talk?" she asks loudly.

I grin. *Finally*.

"Yeah, of course," I tell her, then grab her hand before walking us away from the party.

20.
nia

"She hurt me," I whisper. "She made me rethink everything I thought I knew, and everything that I believed in when it came to you and I."

Cass and I are in his SUV, which is parked in Gerald's driveway. The ear-piercing music is a blurred echo here as the two of us sit facing each other.

"I know she did," Cass tells me. "I know, Nia. But none of what Amanda told you came from me. *None* of it."

"I know that," I state. "I...that's not you, Cass. Everything that Amanda said to me – the threats and the harsh words – that isn't you. It never will be."

"Then why stay away from me for over a *week*?" he asks with open vulnerability. His eyes shine under the lulling evening light as he says, "Your silence almost made me believe that you didn't trust me. That you thought you were better off without me."

"Why didn't *you* reach out, then?" It isn't my place to ask him that, especially because I know he had nothing to do with Amanda's madness. The truth is that I'd let her get in my head pretty bad, and had gotten all fucked up about it. The truth is that I'd taken too long to process and eliminate her insults, which in turn made Cass think I didn't want him.

He pushes back a few errant strands of his long hair. "I don't know?" he voices, shrugging. "Maybe it was because I didn't wanna violate your personal space when you'd just been hurt by someone who was associated with me, or maybe it was because I was too scared to know what your answer would be about everything." He shifts and scratches the back of his head with a thumb. "Honestly, I really don't know why I didn't reach out, Nia. I wasn't even sure whether I was supposed to."

"How long were you planning on waiting?" I ask. "I know you have to leave soon; you can't stay in Adenbrooke forever. So, were you going to leave without talking to me about the whole mess? Were you just going to, I don't know, leave the ends loose and forget about them?"

He frowns. "I literally just told you that none of what my ex-manager said to you had come from me. Why are you questioning me like I'm the one to blame here?"

He's right. Why am I so on-edge with *him*? It's not like he deserves any of this. It isn't like he even deserves to have this conversation with me.

I rub both hands over my face, then cup the back of my neck as I stare at the car's gearshift. "I don't know." I sniff and shake my head.

He places a hand on my knee and gives it a squeeze. "Look, let's just admit that we were both stubborn and didn't want to be the first one to reach out to the other, so we chalked it up to either wanting time to process everything, or thinking that the other person needed space for the same," he says. "Can we just do that, please?"

"Yeah," I agree, then nod. "Yes, let's just do that."

He smiles. "Perfect."

I sigh and grab his hand – the one that's on my knee. "I'm so sorry, Cass," I tell him while looking him in the eye. "I can't get her…*voice* out of my head. Her words just won't leave my mind, and I don't understand why."

"Hey…" He touches my chin. "Come here." He gestures at his front.

I place my hair over one shoulder and rise, only to hiss when my head bumps against the SUV's ceiling.

Cass chuckles, making me scowl.

"I would love to see *you* do it, dick-face," I tell him.

He's laughing now. "Well, you should've made the offer first, then."

I roll my eyes, bend my upper body forward so as to not to hit my head again, and finally manage to straddle him.

"God forbid if I did," I mutter.

He puts his tongue to his cheek. "Excuses, excuses."

I place both forearms over the headrest of his seat and lean in. "Fuck you, Madden."

He smirks as he slowly runs his eyes over me. "Why, hello there."

"Do you not have an off switch?" I ask, then move back.

"Nope," he answers with a *pop*, and when I shake my head at him, he pats my left hip twice and wraps his arms around my waist. "Also, you're stalling."

"Stalling?"

"Mm-hm." He arches a brow. "You don't wanna talk about the effect Amanda has had on you."

I click my tongue and give him my best poker face. "I already told you I can't get her voice outta my head. That's all there is to it."

He narrows his eyes at me. "You sure about that?" he questions.

I clench my jaw as I stare at him, because I kind of hate how easily he can tell that I'm hiding something from him. But I also like it, because it means that he sees me for more than what I choose to show him.

"*Nia…*" he says my name with emphasis, making me click my tongue again.

"I…" I push my hair behind an ear. "I feel like everything she said to me is a reflection of who I've always been, but never found it important enough to acknowledge. And now that she's shown me the mirror, I've been thinking of ways to maybe implement certain changes in my life."

Cass looks utterly shocked by my confession. "Please don't tell me you mean that, Nia. I don't know every bit of the bullshit she spewed at you – only the bits that Noah told me that night – but I know for a fact that none of what she said to you is true."

"And how do you know that?" I ask a little too loudly. "You weren't even there for any of it, dammit!"

"Because *I know you*, okay," he states calmly. "Because I know you, baby, and Amanda doesn't. Because I know your heart, your mind, and your way of living life, and she doesn't. She's a spiteful human being who hides behind her insecurities and fear of failure, and it took years of ignorance and dependence on my part to realize how wrong I was about her, and about everything she represents. It took me losing you, albeit fleetingly, to realize that I'd given her too much liberty over my life and its choices." He lets go of a short breath. "When she told me what she felt for me after I confronted her – it…it made me feel disgusted with myself. I blamed myself for being careless with my words and expressions towards her. I thought that maybe I'd unknowingly led her on. I started questioning the things I stand for, and the kind of man I am. Nia…" He holds my face in his hands. "That's what Amanda does to people: she confuses and hurts and demeans them. That's what she's been doing to my professional competitors for *years*. I know it's wrong that I never really spoke to her about these things, but the truth is that I didn't know how to. This is who she is, and it took me so fucking long to realize what that meant – what her being who she is meant for me, and for the people around me." He touches his forehead to mine. "I'm so, so sorry, N–"

"It's not your fault," I cut him off. "I've known that from the very beginning, but I refused to fully admit to it."

"You had every right to process things and clear your head."

"No, I–"

"*I'm sorry, Nia*," he affirms.

I wrap my fingers around his wrists and run the pad of my thumb over his tattoo, which makes him smile. "*I'm* the one who should apologize, Cass," I say. "*I'm* sorry for giving you the cold shoulder, even though you didn't deserve a single bit of it. *I'm sorry I took Amanda's words so hard that I lost track of you and your transparency towards everything.*"

"Don't." Our noses touch when he cants his head a little. "I get it, I do. I mean, I know firsthand that she's crazy. I just hope she fixes that part of herself before it's too late and she gets herself stuck in something she can't get out of, despite the connections and people at her disposal."

I blink, and when my blues meet his hazels, he smiles again.

"Are you okay?" I ask him. "Like, *really* okay?"

"Are *you*?" he counters.

I chuckle. "Fair enough." I push some of his fallen hair away from his face. "Where is she now?"

He sighs and holds onto me tighter. "Not here, that's for sure."

"The relief on your face is almost comical," I muse.

"I could say the same for *you*," he quips with a raise of his brows. He then grabs my ass and pulls me even closer to him.

I run the back of my left hand over the sharp angle of his cheek. "So, what happens now?"

He presses a long, almost bruising kiss on my lips. "You tell me." Curiosity and worry are clearly visible on his face.

"I don't wanna stay away from you again," I tell him honestly. "I made that mistake 11 years ago, but I won't make it again. And it's because I don't have it in me to go through everything that I went through after you left, Cass. I need you; I can't live without you."

There's a stark hint of surprise on his face, one where his brows furrow and his forehead creases. He grins regardless of it, and I notice how his shoulders relax at my admission.

"God, I can't fucking live without you either, Nia, not anymore." He kisses me again. "But, are you sure you're ready to move so far from Adenbrooke?"

"I wanna try," I answer. "I wanna make things work between us."

"Me too," he says around a smile.

I press my lips to his, and he in turn opens his mouth for me. "Noah is gonna flip when I tell him," I whisper.

"Don't care." Cass kisses me hard enough that I moan and rock my hips against his.

"You should." I move back. "He'll need time to come to terms with the fact that I'll be leaving Adenbrooke. We run the café together, Cass; he's my fucking *brother*. My parents are pretty chill, so I'm sure they'll be open to the idea, but Noah loves me a little too fiercely. He wants nothing but the best for me, yeah, but when he realizes I'm giving up my life here for you, he might have a few things to say about that."

Cass frowns/pouts. I'm not sure which one it is. Either way, it's hilarious.

"What's that supposed to mean?" he asks.

I lift a shoulder. "No offense?"

"Offense fully taken, Miss Connell," he quips, then gives me a cheeky grin. "I'll talk to Noah. We're the best of buds; I'm sure he'll understand."

I tilt my head to the side. "Oh yeah?"

"Pssh, yeah; duh." He waves a hand before him, which makes me laugh.

"If you two really are *the best of buds*, then why did he threaten to punch your teeth in when you came to my house and insisted on talking to me after I ran out of the diner?"

Cass's mouth moves, but no words come out.

"Huh, what was that?" I lean in and put my ear close to his face. "Can you repeat that, please?"

He huffs, and just when I think he's going to reply to me with a snarky comment or something, he moves his hands from my ass to my waist.

"What, have I left you speech–" I stop and yelp when he starts tickling me. "Cass, no!" I try to get off him, but he grabs me before I can, then tickles me harder. "Fucking stop!"

"You wanna taunt me again, Nia?" he says with a smirk. "Go on; give it your best shot."

"You're evil." I push at his chest, but when he doesn't budge, I shift a little and cup his crotch from over his jeans.

Cass sucks in a breath, and his hands immediately stop where they are. "Not fair, Connell," he remarks, "but I like it – a *lot*."

"It's so damn easy to get distracted with you," I tell him with a shake of my head.

He gives me a wink. "Why are you even worried? It's just Noah, babe. I'll talk to him."

"It's not just him." I lean against the steering wheel. "It's about the café and my life here. I've lived it all for so long that I don't know what I'd do without it."

"So, you want change, you want me, and you also want everything you have here in Adenbrooke?"

I shrug. "Maybe?"

Cass chuckles and sits up straighter, which brings us close again. "How about I stay here with you for a few more weeks until you figure and sort everything out? I mean, I'm not exactly in a rush. It's *my* documentary, and I can take however fucking long I want to finalize it. I know what you're about to do is huge, and I'm here for you, Nia, every step of the way. You and I, we'll figure everything out together, tie things up here in Adenbrooke, and then head to New York. Does that sound good to you?"

I blink when my eyes sting, but don't stop my tears from falling down my face. "You'd really do that?"

He flashes a beautiful smile at me. "Why wouldn't I?"

"Your whole life is in New York, Cass. I can't ask you to stay away from it for any longer than you have to."

"Correction: a huge part of my life is here, right in front of me, sitting on my lap. And, because I can't live with only the other half of it, I have to make sure I have it *all* so that I can function properly," he says. When more of my tears fall, he wipes them away and kisses me.

"Why do you have to be so goddamn perfect?" I question. "Why do you have to be so…willing?"

"Because I love you," he answers easily, and my heart all but stops for a moment.

"Wh…what?" It's not like he hasn't said those words to me before, but the last time he had, we'd been 16, and so stupidly infatuated with each other that it was borderline crazy.

"I love you, Nia," Cass says. "And I want to stay in Adenbrooke with you for as long as you need me to. Because I want you to let the unturned rubbles of our past rest, leave them undisturbed, and come with me to New York so that we can build a new empire for ourselves. Because I want you to let me show you why I asked you for a second chance; because I want you to let me prove to you that I'm worthy of you and your trust in me."

"Cass..." My throat is tight with emotions so deep, that it's hard for me to say anything. And I'm afraid that if I do speak, I'll miss something, or that my words won't be enough for what he just said to me.

"What're you thinking?" he asks.

I sniff. "About how well you understand me, and understand my need for time to figure everything out before I go to New York with you."

"Of course. I'd be stupid if I didn't give that to you. It's the least I can do for the sacrifice you're making."

I wrap my arms around his neck. "But is it really a sacrifice if I get to have you all to myself?"

He acts contemplative. "Come to think of it, you're right; I *am* pretty tempting, aren't I?"

I playfully pull at his hair. "No wonder you have such a big head. You need someplace to store all that ego of yours, don't you?"

He snorts. "I'll have you know that I'm a pretty nice guy."

"You're a sunny side up gone rogue, is what you are," I say.

"I don't even know what that means, but I'll take it. Two of 'em, if you will. I'm starving."

I laugh. "Only if you tell me that my idea of wanting to open an outlet for *Café Connell* in NYC isn't a crazy one."

He looks surprised. "You think Noah would want to expand?"

"I'd like to hope so," I state. "I know *I* really want to."

Cass quirks up. "Well, I'm onboard if he is."

I shake my head. "Cass, no–"

"I've already made up my mind, so I'll ask that you save your energy for something else."

"Cass."

"Nia."

"No."

He winks. "Yes."

I exhale. "My savings should be enough for me to get a place for the shop, Cass. And I'm sure when I tell Noah about this, he'll want to pitch in as well."

"No chance. I wanna do this 50-50 in partnership with you. We've got this, Nia – you and I," he says sincerely. "You're willing to live my dream with me by moving miles away from a place that's been your home longer than it has been mine, so the least I can do is share *your* dream by being a small part of it. It'll be my honor, trust me."

I lean in and press my mouth to his. "Thank you." I kiss him again. "Thank you so fucking much, Cass. I love you." Because I do; I really love him. I don't think I ever stopped, to be completely honest.

He smiles against my lips. "And I love you. No thanks needed, Nia, seriously. I'm super excited for you, and damn proud that you're willing to do what you always have, but in a new city. It takes balls, babe."

"I'm scared, though," I admit. "I don't wanna let you down, not after everything you're willing to do to help me bring my idea to life."

"But being scared is good. It shows how invested you are."

"Says the guy with millions of fans around the world," I say.

He chuckles. "I didn't get to where I am overnight, did I?"

He's right. Of *course* he's right.

"You didn't, no," I agree.

"So…" He pulls me closer and runs his nose over my jaw. "How about you ride my cock into dawn as an act of celebration, then?"

I laugh airily. "Seriously?" When he simply grins in response, I laugh harder. "You really don't have an off switch, do you?"

"Not when it comes to you, I don't," he confesses. "I lose my marbles when I'm with you, and I need my fix before I turn into a complete reprobate."

"And would that be so bad? I like to think it'd be perfectly on-brand for you."

He bites the inside of his cheek. "A businesswoman *and* a brand advisor. You're just full of talents, aren't you?"

I tug at his belt and brush my lips over his. "Just fuck me before I change my mind, Cass," I tell him.

He chuckles as he pops open the button of my jeans, then unzips it before sliding a hand between my legs and pushing my underwear to the side. "Aye-aye, ma'am."

The End

ACKNOWLEDGEMENTS

A massive thank you to my ah-mazing and patient beta readers. You know who you are. I love you all so damn much. Thank you for sticking by my side and believing in Cass and Nia's story. You made a difference; please know that.

My family – without whom I would still only be dreaming of writing books, of telling stories. Thank you, Mom, Dad, Qadir, and my lovely aunts.

A cuddly thank you to my bunny, Mickey. You're my baby, and I'm beyond happy to be your momma. Thank you for the endless cuddles, kisses, and sniffs. Those got me through some of the hard times.

My lovely readers, I love you so much. You've stood by me from the beginning, have given my stories a chance, and for that, I'll forever be in your debt. Thank you – from the very bottom of my dramatic heart.

Printed in Great Britain
by Amazon